THE
IMPATIENT
TURTLE

by Jane ___e

Illustrated ___ B___la Mann

January 1997

**Other Janette Oke
Children's Books in this Series:**

SPUNKY'S DIARY
NEW KID IN TOWN
THE PRODIGAL CAT
DUCKTAILS
A COTE OF MANY COLORS
PRAIRIE DOG TOWN
MAURY HAD A LITTLE LAMB
TROUBLE IN A FUR COAT
THIS LITTLE PIG
PORDY'S PRICKLY PROBLEM
WHO'S NEW AT THE ZOO

Published by
Bethel Publishing Company
1819 South Main Street
Elkhart, Indiana 46516

Cover Illustration by
Brenda Mann

Printed in the United States of America

ISBN 0-934998-24-8

Dedicated with a great amount
of love
to our first grandchildren;
Ashley Caroline Oke
born February 21st, 1986
to Terry and Barbara,
and
Nathanael Edward Logan
who joined Marvin and Laurel
on March 2nd, 1986.
Welcome!
We thank God
for your safe arrival
and for the joy
that you have already brought
to the family.

Table of Contents

Chapter One

Beginnings

"The last one in is a rotten potato."

The shrill cry broke into the stillness, cutting the comfortable silence of the hazy, warm summer afternoon. I stirred from my drowsiness. I knew what the call meant. I had heard it often before. The rowdy boys were at the creek again and would soon be storming down the path to slide, jump, streak, or fall down the creek bank and throw themselves into what they called the "swimmin' hole."

I slowly opened my eyes and blinked at the brightness of the blazing sun. I knew that I had to move, and move quickly, but my whole being seemed to protest. This was not the time of day to be hurrying. I blinked again and saw family members and friends resting here or there, faces turned into the sun, arms and legs stretched out as they soaked in the afternoon rays. None of them wanted to move either. I could see it in their faces.

"Dratted boys," grumbled Grandpa Toad, "I wish they could find their own creek."

With that he took a few giant hops and splashed into the creek water and swam under some overhanging greenery.

His action seemed to waken the rest of us. We knew that even now the boys would be scrambling out of pants and shirts, throwing them to hang crazily on bushes, or dropping them on the ground in crumpled heaps. If we didn't move soon it would be too late.

I started for the creek, one slow step after another. Others were moving also. Some quickly, some slowly, but all intent on getting out of the path of the oncoming boys. Though I moved along with the rest of our neighborhood folk, it wasn't because I dreaded the thought of the boys in our area.

No, I didn't share Grandpa Toad's feeling. I quite enjoyed the coming of the boys—though I did sometimes resent their interrupting my afternoon nap. Still, I didn't resent it for long. Their playful games and rambunctious spirit soon had me wide awake and longing to join in the fun. I couldn't of course, so I just hid, out of sight, as close to the action as I dared to be, and watched all that went on.

You wouldn't believe what those boys could do! They ran, they leaped, they dived, they swam, they swung, they pushed, they jumped, they somersaulted—they did everything imaginable on the bank, in the nearby oak tree, on various items they dragged or threw in with them, in the water, and even on one another's backs. What fun they had! And how I envied them!

You see, a turtle isn't too agile you might say. Oh, I can walk forward—slowly. I can even reverse—sort of. But I can't jump, I can't flip, I can't swing, I can't hop. So I carefully watched the boys, hoping to learn just how they did it. I knew by watching that it would be so much fun if only I could figure out just how it was done.

I ambled on toward the water's edge thinking deeply as I tried to hurry. I wasn't even out of the path when they came running, pushing one another, crowding and yelling and scrambling for that coveted first position. No one wanted to be last. I often wondered if the last boy in reality *did* turn into a rotten potato or a rotten egg, or a rotten apple—or a rotten anything. If they did, they must have turned back again, for every time that they came to the creek bank, all boys seemed to be present and accounted for—and in the form of boys.

By some miracle, the tramping, scurrying feet missed me. I ducked my head into my shell for protection. Dust was kicked up in my face and I squished my eyes tightly closed. It got up my nose though and made me sneeze a couple of times, quiet little "Achoos" that made me bump my head on my shell. For a moment I, too, was angry with the scurrying boys. But not for long. How could you stay mad at those who provided such wonderful entertainment? Besides, I could hear them already splashing and playing in the creek water and I hadn't even seen who was today's "rotten" something.

I shook my head to clear it of the trail dust and continued down to the water. It seemed such a long way to go when one was in a hurry. I still had another three feet, at least, and if I didn't hurry, I would miss seeing all the fun.

A loud shriek stopped me mid-stride and a flying boy went swishing over my head, his hands clinging desperately to a long rope. As he swung out over the water, he flung his hands wide apart and dropped with a huge splash right into the middle of the "hole." The other boys all cheered and then another boy scrambled up, dripping wet, to grab the rope and take his turn. Two other boys were playing with a log. I wasn't sure if they were trying to stay on, or trying to get off, but they squealed and hollered and tipped and tramped, their feet traveling nowhere fast, and their arms flailing the air. I knew what the result would eventually be. I had watched it many times before, but I never tired of it.

Two other boys were playing with—or fighting over—a round, rubber, thing. They pushed and shoved and yelled at one another as they ducked under, sat upon, scrambled aboard and fell off of the strange round bouncy thing. It all looked like so much fun that it was hard knowing just which ones to watch.

"Wow," said a voice beside me.

It wasn't until I heard the exclamation that I was aware that I was not alone. It was my best friend, Woodworth, better known as Woodie. "Did you see that?" he continued.

I wasn't quite sure of what he meant by "that," I had seen so many things in such a short time.

"What?" I asked without even turning my head for fear that I might miss something.

"The way he slid down the steep bank on that flat thing and scooted right into the water."

I had missed it and I felt cheated somehow. There was so much to see that you could never see it all. For a moment I wished that the boys would come to the creek one at a time, or else put on their showy acts one after the other or something, so that we wouldn't miss anything. But they never seemed to do that. One just had to watch closely, trying to see as much as possible. It was hard. They moved so quickly from here to there that my neck could hardly turn fast enough to follow them.

"I was watching the fellow on the rope," I said rather glumly to Woodie. "Where's the guy with the slide?"

"Over there on the far side. Right there by the willow tree on that steep slope."

I knew the steep slope. I had been challenged to climb it one day by the creekside bully, Brutus Bullfrog. It had taken me most of the day. Brutus had laughed and laughed. He could manage the slope in a few long jumps. He loved to remind me of it—especially when a number of our friends were standing around. Then he would be off up the slope, showing off his long legs and his jumping skills.

I turned my eyes to the slope now just in time to see the boy climbing aboard the flat thing again and settling himself down, then with a hard push with both of his legs he was off down the slope, and moving faster and faster until he hit the water with a *swish*. He streaked right out onto the water and then seemed to hang for a moment before he dropped out of sight, tipping slightly to his left as his head disappeared beneath the widening circles of foam.

What fun! I couldn't imagine what it would be like to be so—so mobile—so energetic—so lively. How I envied those boys their fun. I wondered as I watched them if they knew just how lucky they were.

"We'd better get out of here."

It was Woodie speaking again.

I realized then that we were still standing in the open, about a foot from the water's edge.

I knew that Woodie was right. We had been warned many times by the elderly of the Creek Bank to hide ourselves when the humans were around. They had some awful stories to tell of things that had been done to woodland or creekside creatures who had dared to expose themselves. I didn't really believe the stories but, reluctantly, I knew that I should pay attention to the advice of my elders.

Without comment I began to resume my walk to the water's edge, Woodie moving along beside me, and we both slipped noiselessly into the cool water and swam to the protection of an overhanging willow.

We couldn't see nearly as well from there. It was annoying. I stretched my neck to the limit trying to get a good look. The boys were still splashing and yelling, though the log had been abandoned now and pushed back up on the bank to keep it safe from floating downstream, for they would want it again. Even the rope hung limp and listless in the slight breeze, forgotten and forlorn. All attention seemed to be given to the newest invention—a slide on the flat thing.

Boys pushed and shoved to line up for turns. Then someone got an idea to water down the slope so that they would slide faster. They didn't have buckets so they scooped water with their hands. By the time that they reached the desired spot most of their water had escaped between their fingers. Still they kept on trying. They even splashed water from where they were, trying to make it fly far enough to wet the steep bank.

Then, one after another, they tried the slide. They had a tremendous time. Down they would go, speeding down the short, steep slope, and then, *ker-splash,* they would hit the creek and soon sink beneath the foaming water, reeling and scrambling and shrieking all the while.

All too soon it ended. "I've gotta git," a boy yelled and the others all looked toward the afternoon sun and seemed to see it as a sign that they had to "git" too. They scrambled up the bank and hurried forward to reclaim their scattered clothes. There was good-natured teasing as they dressed. Someone yelled, "Where's my other sock?" and another boy scrambled through the low willow bushes looking for one shoe, and then they were gone, taking all of their noise, their toys, and the fun of the day, with them.

I heaved a big sigh. Woodie stirred beside me. We waited until the silence of the Creek Bank closed in all around us. I could hear quiet stirrings as creek folk started to move cautiously about again. Soon life would return to normal.

Woodie stirred again. He was waiting for me to make the first move. I didn't feel like moving. I had some thinking to do. Yet I didn't feel like thinking either. I felt a little sad—a little letdown some way. I didn't know how to explain it if Woodie should ask and I was afraid that if I didn't soon move he would start asking, so I forced myself to stir. I would do my thinking later.

"Want to play some water tag?" Woodie asked. I normally enjoyed water tag, but right now, after watching the boys and all of the fun that they had with their various water play, water tag seemed so—so—dull.

"Not right now," I said trying not to let Woodie down. "Maybe later. I'm kinda hungry. I think I'll go look for a snack."

I slid off through the water, propelling myself with my legs. I was a good swimmer— a good swimmer for a turtle, that is. I always won the races that the fellas in my group had just for fun. I was good at water tag, too. I was hardly ever caught and when I was "it" I caught someone else in no time. Still, compared to the long-legged, long-armed boys, I was a nothing.

I moved away from Woodie without even saying, "See ya." For once he didn't follow. Instead he called after me, "When you're done eatin' come on back an' we'll have a game of somethin'."

I kept on going. I wasn't sure where I was going—or what I was going to do. Suddenly I wasn't hungry either.

Chapter Two

Planning

I didn't bother eating. I didn't feel like it. I kept thinking of those boys and all of the fun that they had in the swimming hole. In my mind's eye I could see them running and swinging and sliding and jumping. I could hear the yells and laughter and the teasing as they played together.

I thought of the rope hanging from the tree limb, stirring only slightly as the breeze swayed it upon its anchor on the sturdy branch. I thought of the steep bank that up until now had been a sign of defeat to me. Now it looked enticing and exciting. I thought of the log resting near the water. I had crawled out on that log myself, but only to bask in the summer sun, never to spin and balance and try to throw an opponent into the water.

Well, I wasn't a boy. I was a turtle. Though it didn't seem fair that boys had all of the fun, I knew that there was little use longing to become one. I knew of no way that I could change who I was.

I thought and thought about it, but thinking didn't change anything. I was Pogo Turtle. I couldn't play like a boy. Then another thought came to me and made me feel a little better about myself. I was pretty good at being a turtle—pretty good at leading the local fellas, even if I did say so myself. I guessed that was something to be proud of.

I heaved a big sigh and went to look for Woodie. I was ready for a game now. Even water tag would be better than swimming around alone and in such a forlorn mood.

I found Woodie without much difficulty. He and Snapper and Tubsy and Flip were busy teasing the girls, Sissie and Camma. The girls were trying to build a castle in the sand along the creek and the boys kept pushing the rooms over with their noses. I knew that it wouldn't be long until the girls would be screaming to our parents. Even so, I was tempted to push over at least one room before I took the boys off to play.

"Come on fellas," I called, "let's find some action. This is a bore."

They seemed glad to see me and quite willing to follow me to see what action I had in mind. The girls looked relieved, too. I saw Sissie turn to Camma and say something about "the pests" and heave a big sigh. The boys all started down to the water and just before I joined them, I turned to the sand castle and gave one giant shove with my nose. Almost half of the whole south side went tumbling down and I grinned to myself as Sissie hollered and Camma began to scream for her mamma to come and chase away the mean boys.

I didn't stay any longer but followed the boys down the bank and into the water. Even before we hit the stream there were cries of "Not it," "Not it."

I pretended not to notice. Truth was I wanted to be "it." I wanted to prove to myself—and to show the other fellas—just how good I was in the water. The thought of those boys having so much fun was still rankling me some.

"Pogo's it. Pogo's it," came a chorus of yells. I just grinned and treaded water while I picked out my victim.

I didn't go for an easy tag. I mentally discarded all of the poorer swimmers one by one, my eyes passing over them. Then I noticed Flip. I knew that next to me he was the best swimmer in our pool. He knew it, too. In fact there were rumors that he was practicing daily, on the sly that is, hoping to one day be able to beat me.

Well, it wouldn't be today I determined, and with a quick move, I scooted sideways and swam after Flip.

My move caught him by surprise but even so he was a few feet ahead of me when we started out. I guess that I expected to catch him easily but after just a few strokes I knew that it was going to be tougher than that. Flip must have been practicing all right. He was considerably faster than the last time that I had chased him.

Once I had started chasing Flip I was sort of committed. To turn aside and chase someone else instead would be to concede defeat and I wasn't about to do that, so I pushed hard and kept right on after him. Flip still stayed out there in front of me.

He did a quick maneuver at the side of the hole and evaded me as he looped around and swam strongly back.

I was sure that I would corner him when he came up to the dead tree that leaned out over the creek and rested in the water but he did a smartly done dive right under it and came up on the other side still swimming strong.

It was a bit unnerving to have my superiority challenged. What if Flip should beat me? I gritted my teeth and dived under the log myself and off we were again swimming round and round in the murky waters of the swimming hole, the rest of the fellas cheering us on.

I could hear their cries and shrieks. Our regular group had been joined by some younger fellows, and though my friends cheered loudly for me, a few of the newcomers were rooting for Flip. This, too, irked me and I was even more determined.

Round and round we went. I was sure that the game wasn't too exciting for the others who were present, for with Flip and I determined to outswim one another, no one else was getting a turn. Still, I wouldn't give up. I was determined to catch Flip if it took the rest of the afternoon.

Flip must have been just as determined. I would never have believed that his swimming had improved so. Round and round we went. Down the south bank, round the corner, under the dead tree, through the bulrushes, dipping in and out of the willow's hanging branches, past the oak tree, round the corner, past the cat fish hollow, against the protruding rock and around the corner, to the south bank, and on and on.

I was getting tired. I was hoping that Flip was getting

tired, too. I felt that even the other fellas were getting tired because they were no longer cheering as loudly. I think that they were hoping that the chase would soon be over so that we could move on to something else. Still I pushed on.

I'm not sure if I ever would have caught Flip had he not made a small mistake. It happened as we passed the protruding rock. Now, he knew that rock just as well as I did. We had played on it and around it so many times that we knew well the shape of it. It wasn't exposed above the water, but underneath it was as plain as day. It rounded smoothly for the first half of the way around and then suddenly jutted out another several inches. We used to hide around that projection when we were small and first learning to play underwater hide-and-seek.

Flip must have forgotten about the extension, or else he was just too tired to get around it, for coming around the corner, instead of veering out around, he ran smack into the side of that rock. It must have shook him up some, but he righted himself and kept on going.

But it slowed him down just enough to give me opportunity to give one final push and catch him. A howl went up from the other fellows. I had finally won and now Flip was "it."

We all knew instinctively that Flip was too tired to be "it." He would never have been able to catch anyone, even our poorest swimmer. No one said anything but we all crawled out of the water, onto logs or rocks or the creek bank and Flip and I sprawled out, heaving from the exertion, trying to catch our breath again. For the present, the game was over.

I had won the round but I had been given a real challenge. I thought of Flip and his practicing. He needed watching. I determined as I lay there, eyes half shut, sides heaving, that I'd better do a little practicing of my own if I wanted to stay top dog, so to speak.

The gang wasn't content to let us rest for long. They

weren't tired and they wanted to be moving on to something else.

"Let's go dive off the log," called Tubsy.

I thought again of the boys and the wild way that they played their games. "That's kid stuff," I protested.

Tubsy was quiet.

"Let's go tease Grandpa Toad," offered Snapper.

Now Grandpa Toad, who really wasn't Grandpa to any one of us, had always been a real source of entertainment in the past. We loved to torment him and I was usually the leader. I loved to hear Grandpa Toad rant and rave and believe me, rant and rave he did. But today even that didn't seem like fun.

Because I didn't jump right up and lead the pack, the fellas took that for my negative vote. Though they couldn't understand why Grandpa Toad no longer interested me, they didn't argue. They didn't give any more suggestions either. They didn't want to be vetoed. Everyone was silent, as though waiting for me to come up with some better idea.

I took my time. Fact was, I needed the rest. I pretended to be thinking deeply of something that would really be outrageously fun.

I closed my eyes and tried to slow down my breathing. Silently I wondered if Flip was as tired as I was, but beyond that I wasn't ready to do any thinking at all. I was still too tired. Besides there was no hurry. At the Creek Bank there was always plenty of time.

Chapter Three

An Old Game

The fellas grew a little impatient after a while so I decided that I had rested long enough. I stretched out each leg in turn to make sure that they were still operable, and then I blinked the sun out of my eyes and tried to think. There didn't seem to be much to do except the same old games. The boys were always coming up with something new, like the flat sliding thing. They had never brought that with them to the creek before. And think of the fun that they had with it, too.

I was still a little upset that I hadn't been hatched a boy, but I could do nothing about that. I knew that my friends were all waiting on me for some exciting plan to fill the rest of our day.

I couldn't think of anything. Not at the moment anyway. I stalled for time.

"Are the girls still building sand castles?"

"Naw, they quit."

I pretended to be awfully disappointed as though I had thought of a real good idea for tormenting them at their play.

"Too bad," I said with real emphasis.

I sounded so convincing that Snapper volunteered to go find the girls and suggest that they start sand-castleing again.

"That wouldn't work," I stopped him. "They'd know that we had something planned. We'll just have to wait until another time when they are building again."

I knew by their expressions that all of the fellas hoped that the girls would decide to build sand castles again real soon.

For a moment I thought that I was defeated, then I happened to look out of the corner of my eye and see the duck family as it moved up from downstream to the area of the swimming hole. Here was an old game, but it was fun.

I winked at the fellas and nodded my head.

"Do you see what I see?" I asked casually.

They followed my gaze and one by one, grins began to appear on faces.

"I'll lead," I said, "Woodie you follow. Then Snapper. Then Tubsy. Flip you bring up the rear."

I deliberately put Flip at the end just so that he would be reminded of his proper place. He hadn't beat me yet!

"Move slowly and keep quiet," I warned them. "You know how spooky that ol' drake is."

One by one we moved out quietly, me going first. I slid into the water with hardly a ripple. Once I was under the surface I moved carefully and slowly toward the spot where the mallards were feeding.

I dipped down to the bottom and settled myself while I waited for the other fellas to join me. I didn't want them to miss any of the fun.

When we had all gathered, Flip being the last to form our circle, I nodded my head at the kicking feet above us, and with a grin, began to lift myself up, slowly, slowly, cautiously and carefully. When I was directly under the ducks I carefully selected a pair of small, paddling feet and reached

up and nibbled on the toes. There was a squawk of fright from above and all of the ducks began to swim madly in a circle, beating the water into foam and causing little ripples to spread out further and further.

I allowed myself to sink quietly to the bottom again and grinned at the fellas who were all grinning at me.

We waited until the ducks had quieted down. Then I nodded at Snapper.

He swam silently upward and carefully chose a pair of duckling feet. Edging himself forward, he reached up and gave one a quick little nip.

Again there was a squawk and a flurry of excitement. We could hardly contain our laughter.

It took longer for the ducks to settle down this time. We had to wait and wait until they stopped their fluttering around and returned to feeding.

I finally gave Tubsy the nod and he carefully eased his way upward. He didn't bother with little feet; with great daring he positioned himself directly under the mother. Making sure that we were all watching, he reached up and clamped down firmly on her toe.

What a commotion! We could hear the ducks quacking and calling. The mother was insisting that they should move on, that something sinister was in the pond. The drake was admonishing everyone to be quiet and stop the foolishness. This was the best feeding spot along the creek, he maintained, and there was no reason why they shouldn't stay until they had their fill.

"I've had my fill, now," persisted the mother. "My fill of losing toes to unseen predators."

The ducklings, too, were upset, but it was the drake who won in the end. He quieted them all down and insisted that they had simply snagged a toe on an underground water plant. He told them to be quiet and swim.

We had to go up for a bit of air while all of this was going on. When the drake finally settled his family down and returned to skimming bugs off the surface, we quietly lowered ourselves again and I nodded to the fellas that this was now my turn again and it would be the "biggy."

I was even more cautious than ever. I didn't want anything to scare off that big drake before I had had my fun.

I think that the fellows waiting down below, their eyes glued to the action, must have read my mind. There was not a whisper of a sound or a flutter of movement.

It was hard positioning myself properly. That old drake, with his scolding and his officiousness, kept switching directions on me. I had to alter my course, back and forth and back and forth.

Finally I was in just the right spot and with a quick forward thrust, I reached upward and grabbed the toe of that drake in mid-paddle. What a fuss he made! I guess that he must have believed the others then, that something dangerous and menacing really was in the water, for he lost no time at all in making his departure. I'm not sure if he even waited to see that his family was following him, so hasty was his flight.

Squawking and quacking and screaming out all kinds of threats and insults, he lifted himself from the water and took off for safer feeding grounds. The mother went flying after him, calling out that she had tried all along to tell him so, and one by one the ducklings chattered their way after them.

At the bottom of the pond we had the laugh of our lives. We had to surface so that we could gulp air to enjoy laughing to the full.

Chapter Four

Fun and Games

The boys didn't come to the "swimmin' hole" the next day. I watched for them though I tried not to let the other fellas know that I was watching. I wanted them to think that our games were more exciting than any that the boys might play. I didn't feel that way though and even as I led our group in games and mischief, I still thought about those boys.

I had started the day earlier than usual. While the rest of the creek residents still slept, I peeked out from my shell, stretched my legs, and then crept stealthily to the creek. I wanted to get in some good swimming practice. I had no intention of letting Flip come so close to beating me again.

I had a good swim. I felt in shape and good in the water—but then, I did not have anyone to show me up. Maybe Flip was just as good—or perhaps getting even better. I determined that morning swims would be routine for me from now on.

As the morning sun raised himself out of bed, I finished my exercise and stretched out to dry. It wouldn't do for all of the fellows to know what I was up to.

I hadn't been sunning myself on the log for long when others began to stir.

Woodie found me and blinked with surprise at my early rising.

"Have you already eaten breakfast?" he asked, knowing that I didn't usually sun until my stomach was full.

"Naw," I answered casually. "Thought I'd wait for you. Wasn't too hungry anyway."

With the speaking of the words I realized that I'd told a lie. My tummy was empty and begging to be fed. I changed my words.

"Sure am hungry now though—all of the sudden like. Let's go see what we can find."

Woodie and I ambled off to the creek to look for our breakfast. Fortunately food was plentiful. I was too hungry to be patient in looking for timid bugs or shy worms.

After breakfast we stretched out on the log again to rest while our food digested. By then the creek and the bank were busy with activity. Living things swarmed and buzzed and dipped and sang all around us. I loved the creek when it was bustling with activity and sound.

"What we gonna do today?" Woodie asked drowsily after we had sat for awhile.

"Don't know," I answered. I didn't ask Woodie what he would suggest. I knew that all the fellas expected me to be the leader, and I liked it that way. Instead I said, "I'll think of somethin'. Too early yet. The guys aren't even done eatin' and then they'll need some time to stretch out a bit."

Woodie just nodded.

We waited until the rest of the fellas had all gathered around and then we waited some more while they sunned and stretched and caught a few winks. By then the sun was high in the sky. I had been listening with half an ear and keeping one eye partly open to be alert to the sound of the coming of the boys, but nothing had happened. The day was moving on and we hadn't had any action yet. I knew that it was time for me to make a move.

Tubsy was on the end of the log closest to the creek. I directed my question to him.

"See any fishermen?"

All the guys lifted their heads and winked their eyes open. I could see the questions flashing on their faces. They all were wondering what I had in mind.

Tubsy stretched his neck as far as he could and craned to see down the creek. He started to shake his head. I stopped him.

"Check upstream," I said, knowing that upstream there was a hole that seemed to be the favorite place for fishing.

Tubsy stretched his neck the other way, blinked his eyes against the glare of the sun and studied the prospects upstream. His face lit up and none of us really needed his answer.

"Yeah," he said enthusiastically, "two guys up that way."

I could sense the excitement taking hold of all of them. They began to stir slowly, blinking eyes, working jaws, and even shuffling slightly. Some of them were grinning and they hadn't even heard my plan yet.

I knew that they wanted to ask, but a leader deserves some respect, so they all held back, waiting for the time that I would choose to tell them.

I waited, savoring the moment. When I was sure that I had the total attention of all of them I winked and grinned.

"Seems those fellows are fishing our creek quite regularly." I waited to let the words sink in.

"Not always the same guys; they seem to take turns. New men here all the time." Again I waited.

"They seem to put an awful lot of importance in their fishing." I winked again. Still no one spoke. All eyes watched my face. Now was the time to share my plan, when I had everyone's complete attention.

"Ever seen one of them when they happen to catch one?" I asked.

Several heads nodded.

"They nearly go crazy," I continued. "They jump and yell and wave that long stick around and act like they caught the only fish in the creek and no one else has ever been quite so smart."

Several grins met my remarks. I hesitated. The grins faded. They still hadn't seen where I was leading them. I was glad. I wanted to surprise them with my plan.

I continued to wait, wanting them to make the next move.

Tubsy finally did. He shifted on the log as though he was uncomfortable, licked his lips where the grin had been, and blinked his eyes as though to blink away the fog of his brain.

"So—" he finally stated, letting the word hang in the air.

I knew that all of the others were saying the same word in their minds.

"So," I said, knowing that the time was right. "So—we give them some excitement. If they like to jump and holler and wave their sticks, we'll give them something to jump about."

They grinned again. This grin lasted a little longer than the last one before Snapper asked, "How?"

"Watch me," I said and I pushed myself off the log and waddled down to the water. One by one they all followed.

Chapter Five

The New Game

We all started out for the fishing hole upstream, swimming quietly and slowly, me leading the way. We could have swam faster without alarming the fishermen, but I wanted to enjoy this moment of keeping all of the fellas in suspense.

I sure hope that this works, I said to myself as I swam. I never would have uttered the words out loud. It was tough being a leader and always being depended upon to come up with something that the rest of the fellas thought was worth their while doing. They all loved excitement, but sometimes, it seemed to me, they were a little short on ideas.

I didn't want any of the fellas to doubt that my plan would work so I took on sort of a swaggering attitude to show my self-confidence. I put a sneering, lopsided grin on my face and tried to appear casual and non-caring.

They followed me silently. I knew that they wanted to ask questions—but I was the leader, so they just tagged along, hoping that, as in the past, my idea for fun was a good one.

It wasn't difficult to swim against the current of our small stream. But why hurry, I reasoned. This air of suspense was almost as exciting as the action would be.

When we arrived at the fishing hole I gave the fellas a nod that was to tell them to stay put, and they did, drawing up in a half circle so that they wouldn't miss anything.

I turned to give them one last nod and then nodded again at the lines that hung limply in the water, telling us that at the other end of each was a fisherman. It was always a puzzle to me why they chose to do it this way. If they put such stock in catching a fish, why didn't they just jump in and get one, like the otter or the kingfisher did?

I knew that what I was about to attempt was a bit risky. I had been around enough to know that those hanging lines were dangerous. More than once I had been in the area when a fish, who had been tempted by some goody on the end of the line had bit, and ended up by being grabbed by a hook. By the time the fish had realized that the bait wasn't what it had seemed to be, it had been too late.

I had seen other things hooked too, like old boots, bits of tires, tin cans, or other debris. I had watched as fishermen caught water plants or small branches, and always with the same results. None of them could free themselves and all were hauled to the surface to be disposed of at the fisherman's good pleasure. I had seen some things discarded and left to rot in the sun, while others had been tucked into a canvas bag—never to be seen again.

I was wary of that hook as I moved forward now, though I certainly didn't want the fellas to know that I was being cautious. I looked back and gave them another nod and a grin, just to let them know that I was taking my time simply to toy with the fishermen.

I picked the line closest to me and circled it a couple of times, then I chose a spot well above where I knew the hook to be, and grabbed hold firmly. When I had the line securely in my mouth I moved forward with a lurch and the whole line jerked furiously.

It worked better than I had even dared to hope. With the

jerking of the line we heard shouts and movement above us. What a commotion there was!

"I've got one! I've got one!" a man was screaming.

The line became taut and I pulled back against it, resisting the upward drag.

"It's a big fella," the man yelled again. "He'll really be a panful."

I stole a glance toward the fellas. They were laughing, their eyes shining with the delight of fooling the fisherman. I jerked harder. I braced myself with the help of a broken, twisted branch that lay wedged in the rocks at the bottom of the pool, and jerked again.

"Gonna need some help," the man yelled. "Don't want this one to get away."

There was a lot of scrambling and running around up on the bank. Down under the water, the fellas were holding their sides by now. This was even more fun than teasing the ducks.

I gave another good jerk and was rewarded with shouts and scrapping. Then I opened my mouth and let the line go.

You should have heard those men then! My releasing the line get even more action than my pulling on it had. They stomped and fumed and yelled and fussed, talking all the time about "the biggest one they had ever hooked" getting away from them.

The fellas were almost bursting with the fun of it. I knew that I had really made it big in their eyes this time.

When they finally were able to get themselves back under control, Woodie moved forward. "That was a good one, Pogo," he said. "Can one of us give it a try?"

"Sure," I answered generously. "Give it a try."

"We ought to be up top to see the action," said Snapper.

There was a chorus of agreement. I wished that I had thought of that. I could have positioned them all alongside the creek under the overhanging willows and let them watch, firsthand, what the fishermen were doing as they paraded up and down, flinging arms and waving sticks.

"You all go up and I'll give it a tug," volunteered Woodie.

Eagerly they moved forward. I took charge again.

"One at a time. You'll make too much noise if you all go together."

They stopped, then waited for me to give the nod to who was to be first, and who was to follow. One by one I nodded them up. When I was sure they were all secreted within the hanging branches I turned to Woodie, "You watch that hook now." I wanted him to be aware of the fact that what I had done was dangerous business. Besides that, Woodie was my best friend and I didn't want to see him get hurt.

I followed the other fellas to the surface and took my position among them. Then we waited for the show.

We didn't have to wait for long. Suddenly we saw the line jerk and a fisherman jumped to his feet and started dancing and yelling. Woodie must have jerked it again for the man got even more excited.

"Must be the same one you hooked," he yelled to his partner. "It's a big one all right."

The other man came running and they both took hold of the stick. Then the first man waved the other one back.

"Give me room. Give me room," he was hollering.

They scrambled around some more, sort of fighting over who was going to pull in that big fish. "Must be mine all right," agreed the first man and the second man looked a little pale.

"I guess he belongs to whoever lands him," he said between huffs and puffs.

Woodie gave one more good jerk. The man with the pole nearly fell headlong into the stream. He righted himself and began to struggle with the pole again when it suddenly went slack and the force of his pull flipped the line right out of the water and the man ended up sitting on the creek bank in a rather undignified position, one foot dangling in the water. There was nothing there on the end of his line but the hook with its drowned worm dangling limply from it.

The look on the man's face sent all of us into such spasms of laughter that we could hardly control ourselves. What fun! This beat anything that we had tried yet.

"Can I try? Can I try?" Flip began to beg.

I gave Flip a real cool look. I still hadn't forgotten that he had nearly beat me the day before.

"I think we'd better leave it for now," I said. "We don't want them catching on."

Flip looked disappointed, but he didn't argue. The other fellows looked disappointed too.

"We'll do some more tomorrow," I promised them, and their faces brightened some. I knew that they could hardly wait for tomorrow and another chance at the fishermen.

Chapter Six

Fun or Folly?

The sun wasn't even up the next morning when I heard someone coming down the path to the creek. For a moment I hoped that it might be the boys coming for an early swim. It wasn't. Through the half-light of the early morning I saw that it was two men, fishing sticks in hand. They whispered as they brushed aside low-hanging limbs, "Watch your step. We don't want to make any noise and scare him off."

I couldn't help but wonder who they were talking about. What were they doing here, and why so cautious? I reached over and nudged Woodie. He complained in his sleep and turned over to get away from my poking.

"Woodie," I whispered, bending right toward his ear, "something is going on. Wake up."

Woodie's eyes came open slowly. He saw that it was me and tried harder to shake the fog of sleep from his brain.

"What ya want?" he groaned in a raspy voice. "What's wrong?"

"Nothin's wrong. We might be in for some excitement, that's all."

Now, Woodie never liked to miss anything exciting. He

shook his head again and then began to peer all around in the semi-darkness.

"I don't see anything," he complained.

"They went on—down the path. Two men with their fishing sticks. Said they didn't want to scare something."

Now Woodie was really awake. "Scare what?" he asked.

"I don't know. They didn't say, but they sounded real excited about it."

Woodie poked his head all the way out of his shell and started looking all around. It was still too dark to see much, and the men had already disappeared down the trail, so there was nothing much to look at. Still he seemed excited about the mystery.

"Shall we wake the other fellas?" he asked.

I thought about it for awhile. If nothing much was going on—if it was just a false alarm—then I sure wouldn't want all of the fellas to be wakened early and get mad at me or something. On the other hand, if it was something exciting and we didn't count them in, they might be mad about that. Maybe Woodie and I should just slip away quietly and check it out and then come back for the others if something was really going on.

I was still thinking on it when Woodie spoke up, "Why don't we go have a look and come back for the others if it looks like there might be some fun out there."

That made up my mind for me. I didn't want Woodie to be taking over the leadership role, even if he was my best friend.

"It could be a ways to travel," I said. "We don't know how far upstream those men went. Guess we'd better wake all the guys and take them along. They sure wouldn't want to miss any of the action."

Woodie didn't argue with me.

We made the rounds, waking up one after the other of our friends. It was a tough job. It was still fairly dark out and we had to climb over sticks and rocks to get at them without waking their parents or the rest of the family in the process.

Tubsy nearly ruined it for all of us. He always did wake up with a foggy head. I very nearly decided to leave him right where he was. It would have served him right, too.

"Leave me alone," he hollered when I poked him. I left him for a minute so he'd settle down and then I nudged him again.

"Get outta here," he cried, swatting at me with an angry front leg. His father stirred and poked his head out of the shell just a bit. His big eyes blinked. But he wasn't too wide awake either, and I guess he was used to hearing Tubsy carry on in his sleep.

I couldn't get close enough to Tubsy to whisper in his ear because a younger brother was sleeping next to him. I waited a little longer and then tried again, having already made up my mind that if it didn't work this time, we'd just leave him there.

Even though he was still dopey, he did rouse himself enough to realize that it was me. He still looked sleepy and bewildered by it all, but he did have sense enough to cautiously back his way out from among his family members and follow us silently toward the creek.

When we got out of hearing range, he whispered in a rather loud raspy voice, "What's up? Why we heading out so early? This better be good—getting a guy up so early. Sun's not even up yet!"

"We know that," I hastened to inform him. "We got eyes. Hey, if you don't want to come, just turn around and go back to bed." I was still a little miffed with him.

He was quiet then. He didn't turn around and go home. I guess he could sense the excitement of the other fellas.

We swam upstream to the fishing hole as yesterday because that was the place we expected to see those two men, seeing as they were carrying those two fishing sticks.

Sure enough, they were there when we got there—but so were three other guys. We couldn't believe our eyes. Guess the two men didn't either, because they acted a bit surprised to see someone else already there ahead of them.

Two of the men sitting on the bank were the same two that we had teased the day before.

"Hi, Joe. Al. Getting in some early fishing?"

"Not any earlier than you it looks like," said the short, fat man with the funny hat. "What brings you out so early?"

"Nothing like starting the day with a little morning air," one of the other men responded good-naturedly.

"You guys don't be quiet you're gonna scare all the fish," a third guy said, sounding a little grouchy. They were all quiet then, scattering themselves along the creek bank.

Soon two more joined them. They all seemed surprised to see one another.

We all sat there waiting for something to happen, wondering what was going on. The minutes ticked by. More fishermen came. The sun came up. Others joined them. It was getting very crowded on the banks around the fishing hole. Still we waited. Except for lots of men arriving, nothing seemed to be happening. I was about to give up and head for home in disgust, when one of the men gave it away.

"You sure this was where the big one was?" he whispered to his pal.

"Yeah, I'm sure. Doesn't the fact that everyone else is here tell you that? He mustn't be hungry yet, that's all. You have to be patient when you're fishing for a big one."

So that was it! The two fishermen of the day before had not been able to resist telling around the town about the big one that got away, and now everyone was out to catch the big one for himself.

We looked at one another. I felt rather foolish that I hadn't realized exactly what was going on sooner. I tried to bluff my way a bit.

"Well, fellas," I said, "looks like most everyone has gathered by now. Do you think that it's time for a little fun?"

I winked at them and was about to move forward when I changed my mind.

"Tubsy," I said in a teasing voice. "Are you wide enough awake now to give those guys a bit of a thrill?"

Everyone laughed, like I knew they would, and Tubsy blushed a bit and pulled his head slightly into his shell. He soon came out again, trying to hide his embarrassment, and nodded to me. I could see that he was excited in spite of his feeling of being shamed.

He moved forward slowly and the rest of us chose good positions so that we could catch all of the action. We got it, too. As soon as Tubsy began to pull and jerk on a fishing line, the whole bank came alive. Fishermen were jumping and running and flinging aside their sticks and telling the man what to do and making a grand commotion.

The line went slack again and they all "Oh'd" and "Ah'd" and carried on something awful. We held our sides and laughed.

We let things get back to normal again before we made another move. We were in no hurry. We had all day. We all took turns. It was getting tougher and tougher because the men up top were helping one another tug on the fishing sticks. I was afraid that they were going to pull us right out of the water. We finally ended up by going down by two's and three's, and eventually we all went together. It was harder to all grab the line at the same time and pull in unison but it was the only way that we could give it a real good jerk.

The problem with all of us being down tugging on the line, meant that there was no one up top to see all the fun. We could hear the commotion but that wasn't nearly as much fun as seeing it. Soon we decided to leave just one fellow up top so that we could take turns seeing.

We had to space out the jerking on the lines. We didn't

want the men to get suspicious. The sun climbed high in the sky and then began to dip. Some of the fishermen picked up their sticks and reluctantly went home. Others came to replace them. They all seemed to be determined to be the one to bring in that big fish.

We were getting hungry. We hadn't even stopped to eat, we had been having so much fun. We decided to take a little break and then come back later.

I was a bit afraid that the fishermen would all give up and go home if we didn't keep up the action, but I didn't know the determination of fishermen. After we had eaten our fill, slept awhile in the sun, and then crept back to the creek and swam back upstream, the creek's banks were even busier than before.

Chapter Seven

Trouble!

It was that lovely, quiet time of the day when the sun is almost ready to go to bed and the songbirds are busy singing lullabies to their young. The woods are full of night sounds of creatures going off to bed and other creatures beginning to stir from their full day's sleep. We knew that the men would not stay much later and we also knew that our bedtime was fast approaching, so we wanted to crowd in all of the fun that we could.

I decided to be the first observer. The other fellas went down, noiselessly, and picked the thickest line in the pool to start the proceedings. They braced themselves with the help of some outcropping rocks and on the count of three gave a big jerk.

The shore came alive again. "It's him! It's him," a man was shouting. "I've got him! I've got him! Give me room. Back off. Give me room."

The other men were all shouting that he'd never land him alone, and that they'd be glad to help, and that he had no idea what he was up against, but the man with the pole just waved them all back, shouting, "Give me room. Give me room. Back up some."

I laughed until my sides ached and then I saw the line go slack and a disappointed fisherman had to stand and hear several, "We tried to tell you," "Can't one man land that big fella alone." "See?"

For a moment he looked like he was going to pick up his gear and go home in disgust but I guess the fisherman in him got the best of him, for he was soon putting on another worm and lowering his line again.

Snapper appeared. He was grinning from ear to ear. "We fooled him. Did you see? Did you see how excited he was?"

I assured him that I had seen it all and then, still laughing, I pushed myself off the grassy bank, into the water and went down to help the fellas pull so that we could give Snapper some action to watch.

We repeated the same thing a few times, giving each a turn to watch from above. I was a bit surprised that the fellas didn't seem to tire of the game. Sure it was fun and all, but I had had about enough. I was ready to tell the fellas as much but I could see that Woodie was anxious for one last turn up top so I motioned to the rest of the guys and we went back down to pick out a line.

It was getting pretty dark down under the water now. The lines weren't nearly as easy to see. We chose carefully, certain not to get one that had been recently pulled. We wanted to give all those men up top an equal chance for some excitement.

We positioned ourselves and got set. I guess the other fellas might have been a little tired of the game, too, or else we just couldn't see too well, or we were becoming careless or something, for just as we went to give a big jerk, I heard Snapper holler and knew that something was wrong. We all let go and jerked back—that is, all of us but Snapper. Before we could even do anything we saw him go scooting right straight up and I knew that Snapper was hooked on that

line. A sick feeling went all through me. What in the world would happen to him now?

I had seen the men catch fish and tuck them in their canvas bags. As far as I knew they were never seen again. Is that what would happen to our friend Snapper? I groaned.

Tubsy tugged on my shell.

"We gotta do something," he cried.

I just groaned again.

"They've got Snapper," he prodded me. "We've gotta do something. We can't just let them . . ."

I pushed Tubsy away. I knew that this game had been my idea. I also knew that Snapper must have gotten careless to get caught. I wanted to excuse myself in some way, but I knew that there was no excuse. And anyway, excuses wouldn't save Snapper.

"We've got to help," Tubsy was saying and Flip was swimming around excitedly, agreeing with Tubsy. I had to do something.

"I know—I know," I said. "We'll save him. We'll save him. I have to think."

I was playing for time. There was no way that I knew of to save Snapper from a fisherman. Already I could hear the yelling and stomping on the bank. Already they had discovered a turtle—a small turtle—on their line, not a giant fish.

Flip suddenly swung away from Tubsy and me and headed for the top of the pool.

"Where you going?" I called after him but he didn't even stop, just yelled back, "To see Woodie. He saw it all, he'll know what happened."

Now that was thinking! I hated to admit it but I did—to myself that is. To Tubsy I said, "That's just what I was going to do," and I followed Flip.

When I broke water I saw an excited Woodie and Flip talking together. At first I couldn't make out the words and then I heard Flip say, "He what?"

"He didn't keep him," Woodie insisted, "He looked so mad, he just picked him up, pulled him off the line, and threw him back into the creek."

"Where?" said Flip, sounding both relieved and scared.

"I don't know where. I was so scared. I just saw him throw him that's all. I was afraid he was going to stick him in that canvas sack, but all of the other men were teasing him and laughing and he just took him and . . ."

"We gotta find him," said Flip. "He might need help."

I took over then.

"Tubsy you take the north bank, Flip you take the south, Woodie and I will take the middle."

They didn't stop to argue and we all set off looking for our friend Snapper. I knew that each of us was scared. Scared that he might be hurt badly. Scared that we might be in big trouble. I was also glad. Glad that the fisherman had been mad enough to throw him back. What if he had tucked him in his bag? Then there would have been nothing that we could do.

It was getting dark and it was hard to see. We paddled our way through the murky creek waters calling out for Snapper as we went. I was getting more and more nervous by the minute. I was afraid that we were never going to find him.

Back and forth we went, passing among the rocks and broken tree limbs on the bottom. I was about to give up when I met Mr. Catfish. He had never cared too much for our turtle fun.

"I'd say he had it coming," he threw at me.

I wanted to swing around him and keep right on going, but he blocked my way.

"Couldn't you see for yourselves that those hooks are dangerous. Why a young catfish learns to stay away from them . . ." I didn't want to hear any more.

I turned to leave, but Mr. Catfish slid backward, blocking my way again. His long whiskers twitched. His eyes looked out of the darkness to fasten me where I was.

"He's going to hurt for a few days, you can mark my words," he said. "See that scar there." He pointed to a ragged scar on the left side of his jaw. "Had a hook there when I was little more than a fry. Nearly got me. If I hadn't been so quick I would have ended up in the pan. He's lucky turtle makes poor frying."

"Please," I stammered, "Please, I've got to find him."

"You haven't found him? I can tell you where he is. He crawled up on the bank by that fallen log. I saw him go. He'll be sitting up there nursing a sore mouth I'll wager."

I turned to swim in the direction that he had pointed and this time he did not stop me.

"He'll be mighty sore for the next few days—you can count on that," he called after me. "You youngsters got no business playing around with things you know nothing about."

I knew that he was right but I wasn't going to give him the satisfaction of agreeing with him so I just swam away. I had to find Snapper. I had to know if he was all right. In fact, I wanted to see him and chat with him myself before the other fellas saw him. Maybe I could sort of steer him away from putting the blame on me by scolding him some about his carelessness.

Chapter Eight

Snapper

I wasn't the first one to get to Snapper. Flip found him first. By the time that I got there Flip was holding some cool, soft moss, dipped in creek water, up against the side of Snapper's mouth. Snapper didn't even want to talk so there was no use asking him anything.

He didn't throw any accusations at me and I did not scold him. The truth was I felt pretty sick about it all. Here was my friend, seriously hurt and there was very little that any of us could do to help him.

It wasn't long until Tubsy and Woodie joined us. They arrived all out of breath and started right in to tell Snapper how glad they were to see him and how scared they had been and all, but I motioned for them to keep quiet. They did, but their eyes still looked big and frightened, even in the gathering darkness.

When Flip took the moss away to dip it in the creek water again, I shuddered at the ragged tear that was exposed to our eyes. Snapper had an ugly wound all right. It was still bleeding some, though I was sure that the moss had helped it considerably.

"It's getting late," I reminded all of them. "Our folks are going to wonder where we're at. We better get on home."

"What am I gonna tell 'em?" asked Snapper with a great deal of difficulty. The effort to talk started the tear bleeding some more. Flip moved forward and pressed the moss against it again.

"It's dark," I said. "They likely won't even notice—if we all just keep our mouths shut."

"That might be fine for tonight," said a frightened Woodie, "But morning's going to come again, and what then?"

"Just say—Just say—We've got all night to think of something," I said, a bit annoyed. Why couldn't Snapper come up with his own story? Why did they need to depend on me for everything?

"Come on," I said again. "If we don't hurry and get home we're going to have a lot of explaining to do *tonight*. Our folks won't wait for morning."

Snapper pushed away the moss that Flip was holding. He looked at me and his eyes held a challenge. I knew that he wanted to say something and I also knew that it was going to hurt him to talk. I hoped that the pain would be enough to keep his mouth closed, but it wasn't. He had to talk anyway.

"That's fine—for you. Wait 'til morning. You won't be around when my folks wake up and want to know about this."

"That's right," said Tubsy slowly, "He'll have to face it alone."

"We've got to think of a good story tonight," agreed Woodie.

Snapper nodded his aching jaw.

"How about the truth?"

It was Flip who spoke quietly, never lifting his eyes off the torn jaw of Snapper.

"What do you mean?" I flung at him, swinging around to glare at him for such a dumb suggestion.

But Flip stood his ground, not even drawing his head back into his shell a fraction of an inch. He looked me right in the eye.

"It's not right to lie. You know that! Besides, it's not even smart. He's hurt," he went on. "He's not going to be able to hide it. His folks will see it for themselves. Seems to me that anything that you make up won't make as much sense as the truth does. He got caught by a fishhook! Anyone who looks at him, can accept that. You make up some crazy story—it just won't add up and he'll be in more trouble than he's in now."

Flip spoke very slowly, very calmly, and I knew as I listened to him that he was right. I sure wasn't going to say so, though.

"It's Snapper's mouth," I said with finality. "It's his decision."

That seemed to settle it for all of them. We started the swim back home.

We didn't talk as we traveled.

Personally, I was hoping that everyone would already be settled for the night when we arrived and we wouldn't have to answer any questions. I also hoped that Snapper's jaw would make a miraculous recovery overnight so that we never would need to explain what had happened.

It didn't happen that way.

Our folks were still waiting for us when we arrived and we had to listen to a scolding for being so late. My folks grounded me for the next three days. I don't know what punishment the other fellas received. I wasn't allowed to talk to them—that was part of the grounding.

I heard later that Snapper's folks were plenty upset. They grounded Snapper, too. He did as Flip had suggested and admitted that he had been messing around with fishhooks just to bug the fishermen. They were upset all right, but I think that with his torn-up mouth, they babied him a bit, too. I saw his sisters and brothers scrambling around finding him bugs and things for his breakfast.

I stayed out of the way. I was afraid that Snapper might tell his folks that I was the cause of all his problems, but I guess he never did. At least they never treated me any differently after the accident than they had before.

Those three days sure did pass by slowly. I thought that they'd never end. The boys even came to the swimmin' hole once. I heard their yell, "The last one is a rotten watermelon," and when, without even thinking, I moved forward to go watch all the fun, my father opened his eyes and without even sticking out his head, stopped me in my tracks.

"Where do you think you're going?" he asked. "I didn't know that it was already Thursday."

"I forgot," I apologized, and tucked myself back in my shell again. It was hard to sit there and hear their shouts and squeals as they splashed and romped in the water.

By the time that our grounding had ended and we got together again, Snapper's mouth was beginning to heal. There were scabs where the tear had been, and he still couldn't talk much. He sort of slurred his words, trying not to open his mouth as he spoke. It was hard for him to eat, too, and I was afraid that he'd lose a lot of weight before he was well again.

It should have happened to Tubsy, I said to myself. *He could stand to lose some of that flab.* I glanced at Tubsy, hoping that he couldn't read my thoughts. I guess he couldn't because he looked at me and grinned, glad that we were all back together again, and wondering what I was going to find for us all to do.

I was saved by the sound of tramping feet. The boys were back again.

"The last one in is a rotten turnip," rang out in the lazy afternoon air.

"Let's go see if they have come up with anything new," I

said to the fellas and started off for the creek bank.

By the time we arrived, the boys were already stripped and splashing in the water. Two of them had brought flat, sliding things to use on the steep creek bank. The others insisted on taking their turns, too, and most of the action that day was on that bank.

It did look like fun. Even Snapper seemed to forget his sore mouth for a while as we watched the boys climb up, slide down and go splashing into the water.

"Boy, I wish I could do that," I heard Woodie say. It was exactly what I had been thinking.

I decided to watch them very closely and see if I could figure out just how it could be done.

Chapter Nine

The Slide

"It's simple," I said to Woodie. "You just slide."

Woodie still seemed doubtful. It had taken us a long time to slowly crawl up the steep bank. Now we stood at the top looking down toward the creek water. It looked a long way down.

Down at the bottom waited Tubsy, Flip and the still-hurting Snapper. They were going to wait and see how we made out before venturing up the steep slope.

I'll go first," I said to the hesitant Woodie. "You just do what I do."

I tucked in my tail and legs and drew in my head, leaving only enough sticking out so that I could see what fun I was having, and braced myself for the slide.

Nothing happened.

I wiggled. Still nothing happened. I put out two front legs and gave a push, expecting to go flying down the incline. I didn't move an inch.

Woodie stood looking at me, blinking against the afternoon sun.

"What's wrong?" he asked. "Why aren't you going? You scared?"

"No, I'm not scared," I snapped back. "I just can't slide, that's all. You're going to have to give me a shove to get me started."

Woodie circled around behind me and positioned himself. "Tell me when you're ready," he said.

I tucked all in again and set myself for a good fast ride down the bank.

"Ready," I said, and Woodie heaved himself against me.

There was a bump as Woodie smacked himself right into my shell, and then nothing. I heard Woodie exclaim and start to cry over his banged nose, but he caught himself right away and checked back the tears.

"You didn't do it right," I said to him. "You don't just ram, you push slowly."

Woodie tried again.

It still didn't work. I just sat there right where I was, all tucked in but going nowhere.

"You're not doing it right," I insisted, sure that it would work if done properly. "Here, let me show you how."

Woodie looked doubtful as he took his place. He tucked in his feet and tail, but insisted on leaving his neck out so that he could see just what was going to happen.

"Tuck in your neck," I hollered at him. "You'll break the dumb thing, if you leave it out like that."

Woodie tucked in, though he still left his head out just a bit. That was okay with me. I didn't blame him for wanting to see some of the action.

I got behind Woodie and braced myself for a good shove. He didn't move. I backed up and checked to be sure that he didn't have some feet sticking out somewhere resisting my forward push. I could see no feet. I braced myself again and gave another shove. Still he did not move.

I was determined that I would not be defeated. If the boys could slide down the creek bank then we could, too. I backed up a couple of steps, and with all the momentum

that I could gather I threw all of my weight at Woodie's shell.

With the force of the action I felt myself lift up and hurl through the air. I was sure that I'd break every bone in my body. I landed with a thump that knocked all of the air from my lungs. Not only was I breathless, but I was on my back, a position that I detested. I opened my eyes slowly, expecting to see Woodie swishing down the bank toward the water, but Woodie was nowhere to be seen. It made me panicky.

"Woodie," I yelled, "Get back up here. I need some help."

Boy, he must have just flew, I thought to myself. I didn't even hear the splash as he hit the water.

"Woodie," I called again.

"I'm right here," said a voice just up the bank from me.

I cranked my already crooked neck around to see Woodie sitting exactly where I had left him. He hadn't as much as shuffled forward.

"What happened?" I asked, puzzled by it all.

"Nothing happened," said Woodie, "except to you, that is. You went flying. I never moved."

"Well, help me back on my feet," I complained, waving my feet helplessly in the air.

Woodie shuffled forward and gave a push on my one side.

I rocked on the ridge of my shell. It was an awful feeling. It made me feel dizzy. "Careful," I shouted. "You'll have me rolling all the way down the bank."

Woodie tried again. He was still unsuccessful.

"I need help," he said to me and then he turned and called down the creek bank, "Would one of you guys come up here and help me get Pogo right side up?"

I could have died with embarrassment. Why did he need to yell it out for the whole world to hear?

"Just keep trying," I growled at Woodie.

He tried again but he got nowhere. By now, the rocking back and forth was making me so dizzy that I began to feel

sick to my stomach. And laying on my back with my head hanging down was causing all of the blood to flow to my head. I wasn't sure if I'd be able to tell up from down even after I was flipped back over.

It seemed forever until Flip arrived. I would have thought that even a turtle could have made it up the bank faster than that.

With both of them working together they finally managed to flip me back over so that I could get my feet on the ground. The whole world was spinning round and round and I sat blinking my eyes trying to get things back into proper focus.

"You want to try it again?" asked Woodie innocently, and I could have poked him.

I didn't even bother answering; just started walking a rather wobbly line down the hill. I guess Woodie decided that my answer was "No" because he wasn't long in following me.

As I went I shook my still-whirling head. "It should have worked, I know it. I can't figure out what we did wrong."

And then, in a flash, I had the answer. The boys had poured water on the slope. That was it. We'd leave it for now. It was getting late, but tomorrow we'd pour water all the way down from the top and then it would work for sure.

Chapter Ten

Sliding

As soon as we had breakfasted the next morning, we headed for the creek bank. I was still sure that we would be able to have lots of fun sliding down the steep slope after we had it watered down like the boys had done.

We stood at the bottom, gazing up at the top, thinking about the fun it would be after we had wet it good.

"Who's going to carry the water?" asked Woodie.

"We'll all help."

"We?"

"Sure. We are all going to use it, so it's only fair that we all wet it."

There was silence for a minute, then Woodie asked another question. "How?"

I hadn't thought about that. The boys had carried the water from the creek in shiny pails, after they had made the discovery that their hands leaked too much.

"Maybe they left one of their pails around," I said looking around me.

"Pogo," said Tubsy. "Get with it. The boys have arms—with hands on the end."

"So—?" I said angrily.

"So they can hold onto pails and walk up the hill at the same time."

I wasn't going to give up so easy. "And we've got mouths," I said crossly, " and we don't need them for walking either, do we?"

"No," Tubsy admitted slowly.

"Well, we'll carry the pails in our mouths."

Even as I spoke I knew that it was a big job ahead of us. Flip spoke up. "We can't carry those big pails in our mouths."

"We won't carry those big pails. We'll carry something else."

"What?" they all asked in unison.

"I don't know yet—but give me time. I'll think of something."

I pulled into my shell where it was quieter and I could think, shutting my eyes tightly against the four fellas and all of the other activity of the creek bank. I thought and thought and I still couldn't come up with anything. I could sense the fellas stirring restlessly and I knew that if I didn't soon come out they'd leave me and go off and do something else. I poked out my head. I was just in time to hear Woodie say, "—wondering about using empty shells."

I pretended that I hadn't heard and said rather loudly, "I've got it. We could use empty shells and fill them with water."

"That's just what Woodie said," Tubsy blurted out, "but we thought they'd be too small."

"Too small? First you say the pails are too big and now you say the shells are too small."

"Do you realize how many trips it will take to water the whole slide?" asked Woodie, having given his own idea more careful consideration.

"So? We've got all day." I answered.

That seemed to settle it. We all fanned out and went in search for good-sized shells that could be filled with creek water and carried up the bank to dump on the slope for slipperiness.

Even Snapper thought that he might be able to help, but when he reached down to pick up the shell that he found, he groaned with pain and dropped it again.

"Sorry fellas," he said in his funny new slurring voice, "but you'll have to count me out."

We excused him and he sat at the bottom of the bank nursing his tender jaw.

We all managed to find ourselves a shell, fill them with creek water, and then start our long trip up the bank with the shells held firmly in our mouths.

Tubsy hadn't gone three steps when he dropped his shell. The water spilled out and made a little puddle in front of him. It soaked into the ground and seemed to completely disappear even as we watched it. I knew right away that it was going to take an awful lot of trips before the water we carried had any impact on the creek bank. I didn't say anything, though, and I hoped that the other fellas hadn't noticed.

Tubsy groaned and picked up his shell again and went back for more water. The rest of us continued slowly up the bank.

It seemed to take forever to reach the top. By the time that I got there I was hot and sticky and all out of breath. My mouth ached from gripping the shell so hard, and my legs ached from the long climb. I poured out my water carefully, making sure that it was on the steepest part of the slope so that it would be in the slide area.

Flip crawled forward to dump his shell, too. And then Woodie slowly plodded up to add his. Even with the three of them all together, it didn't make much of a wet spot on the bank.

"Let's hurry for another one," I said to prod them on, for fear that they might already be ready to give up.

We went back down toward the creek again and dipped another shell of water.

It was a long climb down and another longer climb back up. By the time that we got back up the hill, the sun was already high in the sky.

We trudged up the steep slope, puffing and panting and finally managed to reach the top again. I was anxious for us to add our shells of water to what we had poured out before, so that we could see the wet spot begin to take shape. I looked all around, but I couldn't find any wetness.

Woodie looked all around. Flip looked all around. The whole steep bank was dry and dusty.

It was a moment before I would admit the truth. In the time that it took us to travel down to the creek and crawl back up, the sun had already thoroughly dried our little bit of wetness. It was as though we had not poured out our shells at all.

I guess that Woodie and Flip figured it out even before I did, for Woodie dropped his shell right where he was, his disgust showing plainly on his face.

"Wasted effort," was all he said, and he started down the bank again, leaving the shell lay right where it was. I knew that there would be no talking him into hauling more water for the slide.

Quietly I followed him. Flip said nothing, but I heard him coming along behind us.

Tubsy, who was still on his way up the hill, set his shell down so that he could talk. "What's wrong?" he asked. "Where you fellas going? Have you got enough water already?"

"No," hooted Woodie, "and we never will have. The sun dries it out faster than we can haul it."

"You mean we won't be able to slide. Aw, come on guys.

Don't give up so easy."

But Woodie had had enough. He started walking again and as he moved forward he deliberately stuck out a foot and tipped over Tubsy's shell.

Tubsy hollered, really upset over what Woodie had done. I had never seen Woodie act so mean before. It made me realize just how upset he really was.

"What'd ya do that for?" Tubsy was saying in a hurt voice.

"I'll tell you," said Woodie, "it's just no use. I was just saving you a back-breaking trip up that hill." And saying the words, Woodie continued on down the hill with Flip close behind him.

I went too. I wasn't going to hang around and listen to Tubsy whimpering over his spilled water.

"Come on," I told Tubsy, giving him a nod.

"Don't we get to play?" he asked again, still not willing to give it up.

"Sure," I said. "We're just going to wait until the time is right, that's all."

Tubsy turned then and followed me back down the hill.

We all gathered on the grassy bank by the fallen log and stretched out in the sun. Those of us who had been climbing the steep slope were glad for the time of rest. Even Snapper took a long nap without complaining. It was late in the afternoon before we stirred much. We blinked and flexed our muscles and tried to work the cramps out of our legs.

"What we gonna do now?" Tubsy asked. "Is it the right time for fixing the slide yet?"

I had dreaded that question. I looked at the sky, it had clouded over. It gave me a good idea.

"Why should we work so hard hauling water shell by shell, when one good rainstorm can do it all for us?" I asked them.

They grinned and nodded and I knew that they thought that I was pretty smart.

"We'll just let ol' Mother Nature take care of the slide for us," I went on. "No need us working so hard on it. If those boys were as smart as they think they are, they'd leave those pails behind and come to the creek after a rain."

"Yeah," they all agreed. "You have to use your head. Save your back." They were all nodding and grinning and agreeing with me and I felt pretty good about it.

"Use your head to save your heels, I always say," I went on, swaggering a bit with my wisdom.

Again the boys agreed, giving me some big grins.

I still hadn't thought of anything else to do for the rest of the day so I decided to play it safe and put in my piece before one of the fellas asked an embarrassing question.

"I think that we should call it a day early, and get lots of rest, so that tomorrow we'll be all rested up for that slide. The boys never come to the creek when it's raining so we'll have the whole thing to ourselves."

It worked. Everyone thought that was a super idea. They were all for resting so that they would be fresh for the big day tomorrow. We headed for home. I looked at the clouds again. I did hope that they were truly rain clouds and not just dust clouds or something. I'd really be in a fix if the rain didn't come overnight.

It rained all right. I crawled deeper into the dry hollow log where I had gone to bed for the night and tried to shut out the noise of the thunder. Even though I did not like the noise of the storm, I smiled to myself as I thought of that creek bank. It sure would be good for sliding all right.

It was still raining when we awoke the next morning and when I joined the fellas, I could tell that they were all anxious to try out that slide.

I insisted that we have a hearty breakfast first. I told them that we'd need all our energy to enjoy the fun on that slide, but truth was, I was starving. I wasn't used to going to bed so early and it seemed forever since I had put something in my stomach.

We ate in the rain. It didn't bother us much. We didn't mind being wet, though I did hate to stick out my neck and feel the cool wetness run down it and drip into my eyes.

At last we all had enough and with great expectation we headed for the creek bank.

Talk about a lot of "goo"—I had never encountered anything so sticky and messy in all my days. We tried to crawl up, but our feet got all muddy and our tummies dragged in the goo and weighted us down before we put one foot in front of the other.

Water was running down the sides of the bank making little rivulets that spilled into the creek. The rain was still pouring down from overhead and the wind was shaking the dripping trees, spilling water from them as well. Where the slope had been dusty and dry the day before, now it was soggy and wet.

Again and again we tried that hill. We would get so bogged down with the mud that we'd be forced to tumble into the creek to free ourselves of the load. After a dozen or more tries, Woodie flopped down on the wet grass. He was puffing and panting from the exertion. "It's no use," he said, "We'll never make it—not in this mess. We might as well give up."

"You said it," agreed Tubsy, flopping down beside him. "I'm through."

Flip tried one more time. I held my breath for a minute. He looked like he might make it, and then, with mud caked on his feet and splashed up his sides, he too came back down the hill.

"It's a bit messy right now," I agreed, relieved to see Flip fail in his last effort. "Let's wait until the rain stops. A little sun on that slope and it should slide like a wonder."

Heads nodded their agreement and we slithered back to the creek to wash ourselves off. The creek water was already muddy from all of the rain and the soil it carried.

We talked about going to check on the duck family but we didn't see them around. In fact it had been several days since we had seen them in our part of the creek. We had a good laugh over that. We talked about seeing if any fishermen were around, but one black look from Snapper, who still ached from the last time, made us decide to forget about that. Instead we decided to play a little water tag.

I made sure to hit the water first so that I wouldn't be it. I was too tired to want to be chasing Flip, even if Flip was tired, too. I reminded myself that I'd already been forgetting to get up early and get in those extra practices. I'd have to be more careful about that. Lucky for me it was Tubsy who was it and he started out the game by going after Woodie. I relaxed somewhat. I could beat either of them with no problem.

Chapter Eleven

Defeat

It was still raining when we crawled off to bed that night. I looked through the gathering twilight and rainy curtain at the opposite bank of our creek. The rain was still making little rivers of muddy water that ran down the side and spilled into the mud-colored stream. I knew that the bank was slippery as glass. If only there was some way to get to the top. I was sure that it would be great fun sliding down. Why, even the boys had never had a ride like that.

A screaming bluejay flew overhead. I envied him. If only I could fly like that, I'd fly right to the top of that steep embankment. Just think of it—fly up and slide down, fly up and slide down. What fun that would be!

I looked down at my cumbersome shell. I didn't think that I'd be doing any flying for awhile.

The next morning, even before I crawled out from the hollow log where I slept, I could hear the rain pattering on the roof of my home. Would it never stop? I made a face to myself in the darkness. What a dull day this was going to be. I decided to just go back to sleep. But try as I might, sleep would not come.

Even so, I refused to go out and face the day. At least I was warm and dry in the hollow log, even if I was bored.

It was Woodie who coaxed me out, in spite of the weather.

"Pogo," he called. "Pogo, are you still in there?"

I just grunted my answer.

"Pogo. Aren't you coming for breakfast? We've been waiting for you and we're starved. You feeling okay?"

I guess Woodie wasn't used to me not being the first one to want some breakfast.

"I'm fine," I grumbled at Woodie. "Just getting some extra sleep, that's all. Can't a guy even catch up a bit? Breakfast isn't going to run away you know."

Woodie looked apologetic when I crawled slowly out of my log.

"The sky is clearing in the west," he hastened to say. I think that he was just trying to change the subject. "It could be great for sliding this morning."

I looked to the west. There was a patch of blue beginning to show. Maybe Woodie was right. Maybe the day wouldn't be such a waste after all.

I hastened my steps. Woodie seemed to dawdle.

I looked back at him. "C'mon," I said. "If we don't hurry and eat we might miss some time on the hill."

Woodie looked puzzled. Guess he wondered why I was in such a hurry all of the sudden.

We joined the other fellas and went off to find our breakfast. All of us were in a hurry now. We were afraid that the rain might stop before we were finished and we'd miss some sliding time.

That didn't happen. In fact, it was almost noon before the rain actually stopped falling and the sun appeared. We were all lined up at the bottom of the steep bank. As soon as the sun sent it's first rays dancing our way, the fellas all looked at me and I gave them the nod.

We moved forward like we were all part of the same machine and started up that hill with grins on our faces.

The grins didn't stay there for long. The first step told us that things hadn't improved that much. The slope was still gooey and wet. The little rivulets of water were still running down. In fact, one of them had made quite a cut into the side of the bank right where our best slide would have been.

I kept right on plowing through the mud even though I sensed that the other fellas had stopped with the first two or three steps. I was determined to get to the top so that I could have at least one slide down.

It was no use. I got so bogged down in the mud I feared I would never get myself free from it. I might not have either if I hadn't been rescued in a very strange way.

I was trying to turn myself around but I was getting nowhere. With dismay I realized that I was stuck fast in the mud. My face flushed with embarrassment. How could I ever admit to the fellas that their leader had gone and gotten himself stuck in the mud of the bank? How humiliating! I was pondering what to do when I heard Flip holler. I looked up to see what he was yelling about and would have frozen in my tracks, had I not already been frozen in the gooey mud!

Down the stream, arms spreading out and dragging both banks, came a big poplar tree. It must have been downed by the storm and now the swollen waters of the rain-flooded creek were carrying it along with the current. It acted like a giant sweeper, swishing both banks of the stream as it was swept along. All of us were right in it's path.

"Duck, quick!" yelled Flip, and I heard all four turtles hit the water as one. I knew that they wouldn't stop swimming until they reached the bottom, where they would be safe from the massive tree.

But I couldn't duck. I was firmly stuck in the mud of the creek bank.

I had enough presence of mind to tuck in my head. My feet wouldn't tuck. They were too laden down with mud. I closed my eyes tightly. I don't know what good that did, but I guess it made me feel that I was doing something to prepare myself for the jolt, or maybe I just didn't want to see what was going to happen to me.

I didn't have to wait long. A branch of the tree caught me right on my left side and lifted me up out of the mud like I had been walking on dry ground. I guess a little thing like mud doesn't stop flood-power.

I could feel myself swept through the air at a speed that I had never gone before. If I hadn't been so scared, it might have been fun.

Swish, I went. *Swish.* Right down the side of the creek. Leaves were rustling in my ears, the creek was gurgling and gulping, the trunk of the tree thumped and jolted as it banged against rocks and other trees. It was all deafening. I couldn't even hear my own voice as I called, "Help. Help."

I knew there was no use yelling. No one would hear me. And even if they did, there was nothing that anyone could do for me.

We hit some large object in the stream and the tree shuddered and spun around, and I slipped from the branch that was holding me. For one brief moment I dared to think that I might be free, when another sweeping branch gathered me up and I was off again.

I held my breath. My side was hurting. One leg was hurting. I felt that I had been banged and hammered for mile after mile.

And then it all stopped, almost as suddenly as it had started. With a sickening grind and moan the tree wedged itself at the bend in the creek and flopped around like a dying thing for a few moments, tossing and whipping me back and forth. Then it lay still, shivering as though it was suffering.

It took a few minutes before I realized that I was no longer moving. I felt bashed and battered and I didn't know if I would ever be able to move on my own again. I still didn't open my eyes. I was afraid of what I might see.

Nothing happened. Nothing moved. The leaves were still whispering, but they sounded less frightening now. I waited for a few seconds more.

Still nothing seemed to stir. I could hear the creek. It was gurgling and gushing just as before, but its forward movement didn't seem to be affecting me.

At last, slowly, very slowly, I began to put out my head, bit by little bit. Nothing happened. Then I began to open my eyes, slowly, oh, so slowly. The sun was shining. I blinked against the brightness and lay still for a few moments.

Still nothing moved except for the shivering of the leaves on the branches around me.

I opened my eyes all the way. Leaves were all around me. Branches seemed to hem me in. My first thought was one of thankfulness that I had settled on my feet. If I had been deposited on my back, I'd never have been able to free myself.

I sat still and thought about my situation. Moving my head just enough to look around me, I tried to spot a clear path out of the web of tree branches. Off to my right everything seemed to be blocked. I checked the left. To my relief I spotted a little passageway. Certainly it looked big enough for one small turtle to make his way through.

I next turned my attention to me. I seemed to ache all over. Were all my parts still workable? Would my legs still move?

I extended my right front leg, carefully, slowly. It hurt a bit, but it did respond. Then I tried my left front leg. Miraculously, it didn't even hurt; it was fine. I tried my right hind leg. That one really hurt. I grimaced. I was sure something must be broken. I tried again. It moved. It did hurt, but it moved. Then I tried my left hind leg. It, too, moved, though there was some pain involved.

"Okay," I said to myself. "You're still in working order. Let's get out of here."

It was slow work turning myself around in the tangle of leaves and branches, but at last I managed to do so. Then I began to weave my way out of the passageway that I had spotted.

It seemed to take forever and I was tired and sore by the time I was finally clear of the entangling tree. Yet, I knew that if it hadn't been for that tree I would still be stuck back in the mud on the creek bank.

Just before I lowered myself into the creek water I turned to it. "Thanks," I said. "Though you really didn't need to be so rough about it." I counted the aches in my body. They seemed to be without number. "Still, I'm grateful that you got me out—and with the fellas not knowing I was stuck, and all. You won't ever squeal on me, will you?"

For an answer, the tree just waved its branches in the wind and a million little voices began to share their secrets all at once. I couldn't understand a word of it so I just nodded my head and turned back to the creek waters.

Even swimming hurt, though the water felt good on my aching bones. I started back up stream. As far as I was concerned, I had had enough excitement for one day.

Chapter Twelve

Days Of Rest

It was almost dark by the time I got back to our spot by the creek. I pulled myself slowly and painfully from the water and crawled, limping, toward the hollow log that I claimed for my home. As I neared the opening I heard whispery voices.

"Well, someone's got to tell them. I still think that we shouldn't have waited so long." It was Flip's voice.

I stopped, wondering what was happening. Flip sounded worried and upset.

Woodie answered and he sounded like he was crying. He sniffed and fought to control his voice. "He's gone for good. I just know it. There's no way he could survive that—." He couldn't go on. He started to sob again.

"We should have talked to his folks long ago," insisted Flip. "Waiting around won't help a thing."

"But we had to wait and see if he would come back." Tubsy cut in.

"It would take a miracle," persisted Flip.

"Well, miracles do happen—sometimes." Tubsy didn't sound too certain of his own words.

"I'm not saying that a miracle couldn't happen and he could come back, what I'm saying is that his folks should be told that he's missing," said Flip. "They might know about something that could be done to look for Pogo that we haven't thought of. I think we are wrong not to have told them."

Pogo? They were talking about me.

"Never," sobbed Woodie. "Never. We went way down stream and we didn't find a trace of him. That tree will carry him clear to the ocean."

There was another sniff. Tubsy had joined Woodie in his crying over their lost friend.

"We just have to face it," sniffled Tubsy, "Pogo is gone."

"We can't give up yet," Flip said emphatically. "We'll look for him again when it's morning. But we can't let it go any longer without telling his folks."

I was a little annoyed with Flip. Who in their right mind would think that anyone could survive such an ordeal? And why wasn't Flip crying with the rest of them? What kind of a friend was he anyway? I strained to hear more of the conversation.

It was Snapper talking now. His jaw was still sore so he talked only when he felt it was very necessary.

"Flip is right. We have to tell his folks." He was sniffling, too.

I was beginning to enjoy the whole thing. Here I was, attending my own funeral, so to speak. There were my friends on the other side of my log mourning me, and me not even dead yet!

I was glad that they hadn't informed my folks. I'd have to stop them before they made a move to do so, but in the meantime I hoped that they would keep on talking and crying over me. I was beginning to feel pretty good about it.

Woodie spoke again.

"He wasn't such a bad guy. I know he acted a little—a

little—well—arrogant at times but it was just—."

"Arrogant?" said Snapper, and I wondered if he was thinking of the fish hook, "Sometimes he was a nerd."

"He was not," Woodie defended me, "He just liked to have fun. We'd all be sitting around bored to death if it wasn't for Pogo."

Snapper snorted. "Bored—but healthy," he said.

"Cut it out you guys," cut in Flip. "Pogo wasn't perfect but he was our friend. No use cutting him down when he's not even here to defend himself."

The conversation had taken a nasty turn as far as I was concerned. I was much happier when they were sniffling and crying over me. And why did it have to be Flip who defended me? And why did the other guys listen to what he said? Would they rather have him for their leader?

"We'd better get over there and talk to his folks," said Flip. "Boy, do I hate this. His mom will cry and his dad will ask a lot of tough questions—sure that we had something to do with it—and they are bound to yell at us for not telling them sooner—and we should have, too."

"Okay. Okay," said Tubsy. "Blame me if you want. I just thought that we'd find him, that's all. No harm in looking before a body goes and gets himself all messed up in hot water."

There was silence then. I heard some shuffling of feet and a sniffle or two, then Flip asked, "Well, what are we waiting for?"

There was silence again.

"You go ahead, Flip. We'll wait here for you," said Tubsy with a sniff.

"Me?" asked Flip.

"Yeah," agreed Woodie, "No use for all of us going way over there. Someone should stay here by the log just in case Pogo comes home."

"It's your idea," mumbled Snapper.

Flip didn't argue, though I was sure that he felt like it. I heard a rustling sound as he moved slowly forward in the grass of the forest floor and I knew that he was on his way to see my folks.

I could have let him go—just to sort of humble him some, but I knew that I might bc humbled even more than Flip if my folks ever discovered that I had hid while they received news that I was in serious danger. I didn't think they were likely to regard that lightly, so I knew that I had to stop Flip. I moved slowly around the log, careful to groan a lot as I eased myself forward.

Woodie let out a holler that would have raised the dead.

"Pogo," he cried. "Pogo, you all right?"

I groaned again. It wasn't too hard to do. It did still hurt me to walk.

Upon Woodie's cry, Flip looked around to see what was going on, then he wheeled around and came back to us as fast as his short legs would bring him.

"You okay?" he asked anxiously. Even Flip seemed glad to see me.

They all gathered around me and I knew that they wouldn't be satisfied until they had heard my whole story. I didn't bother going back to where I discovered that I was stuck in the mud of the creek bank. No one need ever hear that part. Instead I started with the tree sweeping down the stream and picking me up to take me with it.

I gave careful details about how I was tossed and rolled until I felt sore all over. I told, too, about ending up way down stream at the bend. So far away that I had never been there before. I told about how I had to carefully find my way out of the tangle of tree branches and leaves and how hard it was, and that I'd never have made it if I hadn't had my wits about me. Then I told about the long, slow swim back home, with one leg nearly broken and all the others hurting with each stroke that I took.

They were all saying, "Wow," and "Boy," and "Would you believe it?" and "Just listen to that," to one another, and I was having quite a time for myself. For a moment I felt that all of the sore spots were worth it, and then I went to move forward to emphasize a point I was making and the pain seared through my leg again and I wished that parts of the story weren't quite so true. I was hurt. Really hurt. I began to really feel sorry for myself.

"Shall we go get your folks?" asked Flip.

"Why?" I shot back at him. I was afraid that somehow my folks might think that I had brought this on myself, which I guess I had done in a way, by trying to outdo the other fellas and get up that slope no matter what it would cost me. I quickly changed from being defensive, though, and softened my voice. "Naw," I said, trying to sound big and brave. "Don't say anything to my folks. You know how they worry over silly little things. I'll be okay in a day or two. No use bothering them with it. My mom would just cry and my dad would—"

I stopped myself. I was about to repeat this very thing that I heard Flip say a few minutes before and I sure didn't want the fellas to know that I had been listening.

I knew that they all felt I was really thoughtful and caring to not want to trouble my mother with my aches and pains. Woodie looked at me with admiration in his eyes.

"We'll look after you, Po," he said as a promise. "Don't you worry none. We'll stick right with you until you're feeling fine again."

They did, too. I didn't even have to stir to go get my breakfast. They brought it right to me. They brought me anything else that I wanted too. Oh, I guess I kept them pretty busy for a few days.

I was awfully stiff for awhile, but after a good rest, my aches began to disappear. I didn't hurry them any. No use taking chances on injuring myself further. Besides there was nothing much going on at the creek anyway. The sun had dried up the steep bank again so we couldn't have tried sliding and we weren't allowed to go back to the fishing hole to see if the fishermen were still trying to catch that big fish. The ducks hadn't returned to our part of the creek and the boys hadn't been at the swimmin' hole for several days. Woodie said that he heard them say something about "summer camp," whatever that was.

So, I was quite content to just loaf and nurse my wounds and let the fellas wait on me. Besides it gave them something to do so that they didn't get bored—and it sort of reminded them, too, of just who was their leader. I didn't want anybody getting any crazy ideas about making a change.

Chapter Thirteen

The Creek Bank

I was getting bored just laying around waiting for my body to mend, though I wouldn't have admitted it to the fellas. They were awfully good about waiting on me even though they did heave big sighs occasionally when I asked for something that was a little hard for them to get. They tried, though, you have to credit them with that.

It was getting harder for me to remember to groan when I moved, because I wasn't hurting much anymore, and I had to keep reminding myself that I was still supposed to be an invalid.

I was careful to venture out to the flat rock by the creek daily so that my mom and dad would see me sunning myself. I would call to them as though I was as chipper as ever, and they never seemed to realize that anything was different. Then after they were gone, I'd groan and pull myself slowly back to my log so that the guys could wait on me again.

I guess the fellas thought that I was awfully brave—at least Woodie did. He was always saying things like, "Boy, are you tough, Po," or, "I just don't know how you stand it, Po. You must hurt something awful."

I'd just nod my head and shut my eyes and groan again.

But the fun was sort of going out of it. I was feeling better now and just laying there, trying to think of things that they could do for me, or bring me, was getting rather boring. And then, much to my relief, the boys returned to the swimmin' hole again.

I heard them coming when they were way down the path. They were shrieking and yelling and calling to one another.

Grandpa Toad, who had been sitting in the sun toasting himself, heard them, too. I heard him mumble something under his breath about the "dreaded savages" and then he hopped away in a huff and disappeared under some water-lily leaves.

Then I heard, "The last one in is a rotten cabbage," and I knew that they were already on the bank.

The fellas heard them, too. They had all been out rustling me up some fresh clover roots when the boys put in their appearance. They all came back huffing and puffing, afraid that I might miss it all if they weren't around to tell me about it, though it's beyond me how anyone in our quarter of the globe could have missed the sound of those boys.

"They're back, Pogo. The boys are back at the swimmin' hole," panted Woodie.

I nodded slowly, not wanting to seem too energetic.

Tubsy looked sad. "It's a shame you gotta miss them," he said, "knowing how much you like watching them."

I nodded again, wondering just how I was going to handle this.

"We could help you move to the flat rock," put in Woodie, "just like we do so you can say Hi to your folks."

"That would be good of you, Wood," I said, giving Woodie a well-deserved grin.

He flushed some.

They moved to help me.

"I am commencing to feel a bit better," I admitted. "You

fellas have sure taken good care of me. I'm hoping that in a day or so, I'll be able to get along on my own."

That was good news to all of them. They cheered for good ol' Po.

We moved to the flat rock, the fellas helping me some, and Flip hurrying on ahead to brush aside any rough stones or pieces of stick that might be in my path. I forced myself to move slowly, when I really wanted to go my fastest. It was hard to do. I was afraid that I might miss some new trick of the boys. I didn't know anything about "summer camp" but if it was a place where boys went, then perhaps they would have learned something new to try while they were there.

By the time I was eased up onto the flat rock, all of the boys were in the water. There was much splashing and frenzied activity. Still, I was a bit disappointed at first. It seemed that they were just doing all of the same old tricks.

They had their flat things and their pails again, and after they had played for awhile in the cool creek water, they began to carry their pails of water up the steep slope and splash it carelessly over the ground. The rain had rutted the best path down the steep bank and two of the boys went down on their knees while they patched and patted the area to make it smooth again. When they were satisfied that it was okay they started sloshing water again.

It took them quite a while before they were satisfied with the slope. Then they dragged the flat thing up the hill and one sat on it while the other gave him a shove. Down he came, swishing right down the slope and splash into the water.

They all yelled a lot. The one who rode the flat thing yelled because he was having a good ride. The one who pushed him yelled because he had given a good push. The ones in the water yelled, too, but I don't really know their reason. Maybe they just liked to yell.

Up and down they went, one after another, and then they

started all over again and each had another turn, and another and another. It seemed that they never got tired of the game.

I didn't get tired of watching them either. It looked like so much fun. I longed to be able to try it myself. And then I got a great idea.

As soon as the boys left, the hill would be ours. It wouldn't be too rainy or too dry because the boys had made it just right. Every now and then they would slosh on another pail of water, just to keep it slippery. I could hardly wait now for the boys to go home.

The fellas were all enjoying watching the boys almost as much as I was. I could feel the tension all around me and I knew that each one of them was sitting there envying those boys. I said nothing. I would spring it as a surprise.

At last the boys looked at the sky, yelled to one another with a different kind of yell, and scrambled out of the water to sort out their clothes. We watched them go, still yelling and pushing and then I turned to the fellas, excitement in my voice.

"Are you fellas ready for some fun?" I asked them.

"Sure," they answered all together, but they looked puzzled.

"See that hill?" I said, "The boys left it just right for sliding."

They all looked at the hill and then they started to grin.

Then Woodie looked back at me with a sad look on his face. "You guys go ahead," he said, "I'll stay here with my buddy, Po."

"We'll take turns staying with him," volunteered Tubsy. He sounded so patronizing—so martyr-like.

I stumbled for words, wondering how I was going to get myself out of the jam and up that hill for some fun.

"Hey, fellas," I said, "I appreciate what you're doing for me, but I wouldn't have you miss the fun for anything.

We've waited weeks for this. Now we're all going to do it together. It won't hurt too much. I think I'll be able to pull myself up that hill—if I take it slow and easy."

They all began to talk at once, even Snapper, whose jaw was now almost as good as new. They started telling me that I shouldn't take such chances, and that I'd hurt real bad, and that they wouldn't let me take any risks just so that they could have fun. They didn't mind missing out on it for a pal, they went on, and all that stuff.

I still insisted. "I'll go slow. I'll take it easy, I promise," I kept saying. "You fellas have already missed a lot of fun in the last few days while you've been taking such good care of me. Now stop arguing and let me do something for you for a change."

It took a lot of talking and I was afraid for a moment that it wasn't going to work, but finally they agreed that I could go up the hill, if I went slowly, and let them boost me a bit up the steepest part, and took it really easy when I reached the top.

We started up. In my excitement to reach the top and that slide I sort of forgot myself and climbed faster than any of the rest of them. I guess they sort of forgot in their excitement, too, because nobody said anything.

When we finally all got to the top we were breathless and should have taken some time for a rest, but we were all too excited about the ride down.

"Who's first? Who's first?" they were all asking.

I cleared my throat.

"Seeing I'm already sort of banged-up," I volunteered, "maybe I should try it. Just in case anything goes wrong. I wouldn't want one of you other fellas hurt, too."

I could tell that Woodie thought I was all heart. Flip looked a little doubtful, but he held his tongue.

I took my place on the brow of the hill and tucked myself carefully in.

"You have to give a push," I said. "I watched the boys. They always gave a push."

"Say when you're ready," chirped Tubsy, his voice high with excitement.

I rearranged my legs a bit, opened my eyes just a fraction so I could see, and then said, "Ready."

As one they all gave a shove. I humped forward and then settled right back where I had been before. Snapper bumped his nose on the back of my shell and it started to bleed. It wasn't a bad nose bleed but Tubsy had always been squeamish about blood. He squealed like Snapper was bleeding to death and I had an awful time getting him to settle down.

When the commotion subsided we got settled again. I tucked in and the three remaining fellas—Woodie, Tubsy and Flip—got ready to push. Snapper was still sitting off by himself nursing his sore nose.

They gave another big heave. I still didn't move but Woodie slipped in the mud and skinned his knee on a sharp stone. I was afraid that I was going to lose all of my pushers.

"You're doing it all wrong. The boys don't do it that way." I argued.

"The boys don't have to push with their noses," Flip stated.

I let the remark pass and tried to explain how they should push.

We tried it again but the results were no better than before.

"We need something flat," said Flip. "The boys don't just sit down and slide. They have something flat that slides easy."

I hated it when Flip thought faster than I did.

"That's just what I was about to say," I said. "Let's find something flat."

We all started looking. The first thing that we found was a piece of flat rock. It took a good deal of effort to get it pushed into place and then I crawled aboard and settled myself, ready for a great ride.

"Ready," I called, and the boys gave a big shove. I was moving. I opened my eyes to catch the beauty of the ride and then "plop"—I stopped short. I had only slid across the flat rock and dropped into the mud again.

We next tried a large flat leaf. That didn't work either. It just buried itself in the mud and sat there.

The wetness was quickly drying in the afternoon sun and we still hadn't been able to get down the hill. The fellas were getting tired with pushing and I was getting impatient with getting ready and never going anywhere.

"I've got it," I cried in desperation. "My shell."

"What?" said three incredulous voices.

"My shell. I think that it would slide."

"Your shell? You'd have to be upside down to—."

"That's what I mean. Flip me over."

"Aw c'mon Po," said Woodie, "you know you hate being on your back."

"This will be different," I continued. "I'll just be on my back while I slide down the hill and as soon as I hit the water I'll be right side up again."

They all looked doubtful, but I insisted. "Turn me over. It'll work. I'm sure it'll work."

I tucked all in and they nudged me over. Woodie was right. I did hate being on my back, but I sure wasn't going to say so.

"Now push," I yelled out to them.

They pushed.

It worked, I started to slide down the hill. I felt like I was whirling along. I didn't even dare to open my eyes to see just how fast I was going. I heard cheers behind me on the hillside.

There was one thing that I hadn't thought about. I could not see where I was going, not that it would have done me

any good, for I realized, too late, that I had no way to steer myself.

I kept going faster and faster—and then the cheers at the top of the slope turned to frantic yells and the next thing I knew I was flying through the air like a bird.

Now I had always wanted to be able to fly, but deep within me something told me that there was something all wrong with this. A bird knew when and where to land when the flight was over. I knew nothing. I remember thinking that I sure hoped I'd hit water when I came down, but I didn't. I'm not sure what it was that I did hit. Whatever it was, it knocked the breath right out of me and left me groaning again, and this time for real.

I didn't even know if I was right-side-up or upside-down. I really didn't care. All I wanted was to breath again.

It seemed forever before the fellas got there and then they put their shoulders to my shell and got me right-side-up again. I think that they were all scared half to death.

"Po!" said Woodie, with coaxing in his voice. "Pogo. Are you okay? Say something. Po."

I groaned and blinked my eyes. It was the best thing I could do, but it seemed to make the fellas feel somewhat better.

I was breathing again and the world was starting to turn back to it's proper color and dimension. I opened my eyes again and groaned one more time.

"Are you okay, Pogo?" asked Flip.

I tried to move my head. My neck still was attached to my body and my head to my neck. I was glad of that. One by one I tried my legs. They all still worked. "Yeah," I groaned slowly, "Yeah, I'm all right."

They all seemd to sigh together.

"Boy were we scared," admitted Tubsy. "We thought you'd get smashed to bits."

I was rather proud of myself in spite of it all. I had slid

down the bank. Oh, maybe not the way that the boys did, but I had sure slid. I grinned and tried to move a stiff leg.

"I did it," I said winking at them. "I told you I could, didn't I? Boy, did I fly, or what?"

The boys sent up a cheer that made my day. I flew all right.

I grinned, a crooked grin, my head still spinning, then I started for the creek.

I wasn't saying so, but there was nobody, I mean nobody, who could have talked me into trying that again.

Chapter Fourteen

The Rope

I spent most of the next day recuperating from my fast trip down the hillside and my smash into the big rock on the shore of the creek. I had to listen to the boys describe my ride over and over again. I even had to pretend that I had enjoyed it. But when Woodie suggested that we climb the bank and try it again, I had to think quickly for some way to veto it.

"It's all dried out now," I hastened. "I don't think that it would work."

The fellas all looked disappointed.

"Maybe the boys will come back and water it again," said Tubsy hopefully.

I almost groaned. With all my heart I hoped not.

We did make it through the day without the boys coming back and I went to bed thankful that I was saved from admitting my fear of·that hill.

The next day I heard the boys coming and was about to duck out a back way and go to the creek and hide among the marsh grasses, but I wasn't quick enough. There were Woodie and Tubsy, all excited.

"They're back," they shouted. "They're back! Now we can play on the hill again."

I tried to grin but the horror of that lightning-fast, blind ride down the steep bank haunted me.

"Let's go watch. Let's go watch," pleaded Tubsy, so excited that he sort of bounced up and down—which is hard for a turtle.

We headed for our flat rock. Flip and Snapper met us there. They were already positioned on the rock where they would have a good view of the proceedings. Flip moved over to give me my choice spot without saying anything, but I wondered if he really would have preferred to keep it for himself.

The first few minutes went much as usual. The boys frolicked in the water, splashed one another, pulled one another under, and kicked and screamed to be let up again.

It was rather interesting to watch, but I hoped that they would soon get on with the good stuff.

Much to my relief I didn't see any flat things. I didn't see any pails either, and thought all that they might do would be to fight and squeal. Then the biggest boy, whom I suppose was their leader, crawled out of the water and took hold of the rope that was swinging gently in the breeze as it dangled from the big oak tree on the bank.

He grabbed the rope and swam to the other side of the creek. Then he took a firm hold, gave a big push with his feet and swung out over the water, right to the middle of the hole, where he dropped *kersplash* right among all of those other boys. I had never seen such a big splash. The water flew sky high. The waves tossed up on the shore. The rock that balanced on the side of the bank seemed to teeter back and forth.

It was marvelous. I guess the boys thought so too, for they all began to clamor for the rope. By some strange rule that I couldn't understand, someone gained possession of it and swam across the creek to where the other boy had stood. Then he too grabbed a good hold, gave a big shove, tucked up his feet and went swinging out to the middle where he dropped amid shouts and cheers.

This looked like even more fun than the sliding had been. I squinted my eyes against the bright sun so that I could see exactly how they did it. Swim. Grab. Push and tuck. That's all there was to it. Swim. Grab. Push and tuck. I memorized each of the movements as I watched one after the other of the boys try it. It worked the same every time.

I could hardly wait for the boys to leave again. This would be a cinch. Why, there wasn't even any risk involved. Any turtle could swim. And any turtle could grab. And any turtle could push and tuck. I was just sure that we'd have the time of our lives.

I wasn't worried about them taking the rope. The rope had hung on that old oak tree for years as far as I knew. The boys had swung on it many times before, but they had never crossed the creek and swung back with it like they did today. I could hardly wait to give it a try.

At last the boys did crawl out and get dressed. Even before they left the creek bank I started talking.

"Hey, fellas," I said. "We can do that."

"Do what?" asked Tubsy, not following me.

"Swing like that. Drop out in the middle. Didn't you see them?"

"Sure we saw them," said Snapper. "Course we saw them."

"Well," I prompted, "wouldn't you like to give it a try?"

"Sure I would," said Snapper. "Sure I would—if I were a boy."

It made me angry. It just wasn't fair. Why should boys have all the fun? Why shouldn't turtles be able to do something besides catch bugs and sit in the sun? It just wasn't fair at all.

"Sit here if you want to. Sit your whole life away—but I'm going to try it."

"Just a minute, Pogo," said Flip, in a consoling voice. "Sure we want to try new things. We like to have fun, too, but remember what happened on the steep bank yesterday. You could have been killed when you flew into that rock."

I wasn't going to listen. Not to Flip—not to anybody.

"Well, maybe I might as well be dead as to sit here—like a—like a bump, day after day. What kind of a life is that?"

No one answered me. I pushed myself off the rock and started for the dangling rope. They all followed me. Somehow I had known that they would.

No one said anything until we reached the rope. It was much thicker than I had thought it to be. I stood thinking about how I would get the heavy thing in my mouth when Woodie asked, "How you going to hold it Po? You don't have hands like the boys."

"Who said you need hands?" I snapped at my best friend. "Watch me."

And saying this, I leaned forward and took the rope firmly in my mouth.

I started for the creek but was jerked up short. I had forgotten to leave enough slack in the rope to let it cross the water.

I dropped it and walked farther down toward the end of it. When I thought that I had allowed enough rope for it to cross the creek, I grabbed it again and started out.

It was heavier and more cumbersome than I had thought. Even though I managed to drag it to the waters' edge I found it hard to swim with. And then my friends joined me. Woodie and Tubsy each grabbed the rope in their mouths as well and with three of us tugging we got it to the other shore.

Snapper and Flip were just behind us. We all crawled ashore and I couldn't help being pleased with myself. I had gotten this far, there was nothing stopping me now.

"You just give the orders, Po," Woodie said. "We'll do whatever you say."

Great little guy, Woodie. Nobody could wish for a better follower.

"Just hold the rope steady so I can get a good grip," I told them.

They did, all four of them latching onto it at one place or another. I couldn't even get near it.

"You've got to give me room to get at it," I informed them, rather testily. "Here, Woodie, you and Flip hold it. Tubsy and Snapper, just back up a bit."

We finally got organized.

I knew that I wouldn't be able to talk once I got the rope in my mouth, so I gave them my instructions before hand.

"Watch me. When I get a firm hold, I'll wink. Then you let go and get out of the way."

They nodded.

I hoisted myself up on my hind legs, reached as far up the rope as my neck would stretch and took a firm hold. I tugged on it a couple of times just to make sure that it wouldn't slip and then winked an eye at the fellas.

They both let the rope fall from their mouths and stepped back quickly. Woodie stepped too quickly. He tripped over the dangling end of the rope that was trailing on the ground behind him and the weight of his whole body flipped the rope where I was hanging, flipping me, too. The sharp jerk pulled the rope from me, feeling like it would tear my jaw from my face. I spun in the air and landed with a *thud*.

Slowly I pulled myself up, annoyed and frustrated. The rope had swung on across the creek without me. We had to start all over again.

It took us a long time to get the rope back over to the right side of the creek again, and then we all took our positions. I was careful to make sure that Woodie wasn't all wrapped up in the rope again. Red-faced, he held tight to the heavy cord as I heaved myself up and took a firm hold again.

Nothing happened.

Now I was sure that we had the "swim" and "grab" part right. The "push and tuck" didn't turn out to be as easy as it had looked.

I tried to push. There was nothing to push against, and I couldn't tuck until I had pushed. I waved a leg until I got the attention of the fellas. Somehow they understood that I wanted them to grab the rope again.

When they had a firm hold so that I could let go without fear of it flying back across the creek again, I stepped back.

"This isn't going to work," I told them. "I can't push hard enough. You're going to have to give me a shove."

"Maybe it would work better if you stood on that rock," said Snapper from the sideline where he had been watching it all.

I looked at the rock. It had proved itself to be my enemy the day before, but today, perhaps it could be my friend. It was a big one that was perched on the very edge of the creek. It would be a good launching pad. I nodded to Woodie and Flip and they helped me drag the rope to the rock and clamber up on it.

Then we had to go through all of the difficult maneuver again. Each of us knew what to do now, so the fellas grabbed the rope and held it steady until I got myself in position and got a good hold, and then at my wink, they stepped back hurriedly and each gave a big shove.

I was airborne! It was working all right. I went flying right off that rock and out through space. It was quite a sensation to swing through the air at such a speed. My teeth clamped firmly on the rope, and I felt it pull me out and away.

My problem was I didn't know quite how to let go, and as I swung out over the middle of the creek where I should have fallen into the deep swimmin' hole, I still hung on.

I was traveling right on, heading for the bank on the other

side, and the big oak tree.

"Let go! Let go!" I heard someone yelling, but for some reason my mouth just wouldn't open and release that rope. Right ahead was the oak. I could feel it coming.

I was on the ground when I woke up. My side hurt, my back hurt, my neck hurt. I hurt all over. Flip and Woodie were bending over me and Tubsy was crying in the distance somewhere. Snapper came forward with a dripping-wet bit of woodland moss and pressed it firmly against my brow.

"He's coming to," said Flip. "I think he's coming to."

"You okay, Po?" Woodie was asking in a frightened voice. I wondered just how many times I had heard those words from him.

I groaned and lifted my head. Boy, did I have a headache.

"You okay?" It was Woodie again.

"I'm okay," I tried to say, but the words didn't come out quite right. "Just need to rest," I mumbled. "Be okay in a minute."

"He's gonna kill himself for sure, with his fool stunts," I heard Snapper say softly, "Those kinds of things aren't for turtles to be trying. You need arms and legs too—" But Flip hushed him up.

Maybe they were right. Maybe I—but I couldn't think straight. Any thinking that had to be done would just have to wait.

"I'm okay guys," I managed. "Fine. Just leave me. Okay? I'll be fine. Need some rest now. See you later."

They didn't appear to be too convinced. They still sort of hung around for awhile. It was Flip who finally talked them into leaving.

"We'd better let him rest," he said. "We'll check back now and then to be sure he's okay. C'mon."

They all left me and I put my aching head down on the soft grass, feeling thankful to still be in one piece.

Chapter Fifteen

Thinking It Through

I was mighty sore the next day. I didn't feel up to doing much. I didn't feel like talking either, so when the fellas came around I just pretended that I was asleep and they soon left again.

Truth was that I was doing a lot of thinking.

It didn't seem at all fair to me that a turtle should miss out on all of the fun things in life. Birds could fly and dip and soar. Rabbits could race and hop and run. Squirrels could climb and chatter and jump. And boys—well boys could do almost anything. It just didn't seem fair.

I looked down at my legs. They weren't long legs, but they were good legs. Why couldn't they jump? Why couldn't they climb? They couldn't even run. All that they could do was to walk—very slowly.

I looked at my front. There wasn't much of me that even showed. All of me was tucked away in the shell that my mom laughingly called my "motor home." Well, I didn't want a motor home. I wanted a body that could move quickly, that could hold things, that could swing or fly or climb. I looked at the shell again. And then I understood clearly. My *shell* was my problem. That was why I wasn't able to do all of those things that other creatures could.

Did a squirrel have a shell? No. Could he have climbed up a tree in a flash if he was carrying a shell on his back? Of course not.

Did a rabbit have a shell? No. Could he have hopped and ducked and played hide and seek if he were all shut up in a shell? Never!

Did a bird have a shell? I'd never seen a one with a shell, even though I had seen many kinds of birds. Could a bird wing its way up near the clouds, and dip after dragonflies or land on the topmost branch with a shell? There's no way!

Then that was it! It was my *shell* that was the problem. Without it, who knew what I might be able to do?

I began to wonder just what kind of a body I had under the shell. Was I covered with fur like the rabbit or squirrel or was I feathered like a bird? Maybe I was smooth and fair like the boys, and would have to wear clothes to keep me warm.

I liked the idea of looking like a boy. I liked the idea of being able to change my color everytime that I got dressed to go out. I decided that under my shell I would probably look like a boy. No fur or feathers. After all, my legs did not have fur or feathers, nor did my neck.

"Who knows," I said to myself, "if I could just get rid of this shell I might be able to do all of the things that a boy can do."

The problem then seemed to be finding some way to get the miserable shell off my back. It was keeping me down. It was holding me back. It was preventing me from being the kind of being that I could be.

Woodie came to see me. I didn't dare tell him what I was thinking. Besides, I wanted to keep it as a surprise. Just think what it would be like to go swinging through the air on the rope and splash into the water, or go sliding down the slope on the flat thing. Then I could call out to the other fellas, "Hey, fellas. It's me, Pogo. Don't you recognize me without the shell? Hey, I got *rid* of that thing. It was too confining." Then they would all look at me in amazement and envy, and, just to be a great friend, I'd show them how to get rid of their shells too, much to the wonder of all of the other turtles in the creek.

But I didn't say any of this to Woodie. He might not understand—yet. Instead I said, "Woodie, would you do me a favor?"

"Sure," said Woodie. He was always ready to do a favor for his best friend, Pogo.

"I want you to take a real good look at my shell."

"Did you hurt it when you smashed into the tree?" he asked in alarm.

I couldn't tell Woodie that I wished I had busted the thing clear off of me. Instead I said, "Naw, I'm all right. I just want to know how it's fastened on, that's all."

Woodie looked puzzled, but he started to look me over.

"See any hinges?" I asked.

"No hinges," said Woodie.

"Any zippers?"

"Zippers? No, no zippers." answered Woodie.

"No buttons, or snaps or hooks or anything?"

"Nothing."

"It looks like it's on for good, huh?"

"Looks good and solid to me. Why you asking? Is it feeling loose, or funny or something?" asked Woodie.

"No, nothing like that. Feels the same as ever. Just wondering, that's all."

Woodie shook his head. He didn't stay long. Later I heard him talking to Flip. "I'm really worried about Pogo," he said. "He might have hit his head even harder than we thought. He sure is saying some weird things."

I didn't pay any attention to him. I was still trying to come up with a way to get rid of my shell. If it didn't hook, or button, or zipper, or hinge on, then it was pretty solid all right and it seemed that the only way to get it off was to break out of it. But how?

I thought about it all that day and the next and I still didn't think of a way.

I looked down at my shell. If it wasn't for *it* I could be having lots of fun like other creatures. Why should my shell keep me slow and pokey, when my body inside wanted to race and run and soar? It wasn't fair! It wasn't fair at all!

I went to bed angry and upset. I had found the source of my problem, but I was no nearer to the solution. It seemed that there was just no way for me to rid myself of my hateful shell and free myself for adventures.

The next morning I decided that I didn't want to see my friends. I knew that they would be around to see how I was feeling and now that I was looking better, they would expect me to go right on doing all those silly, boring things that we were confined to doing. Well, I wouldn't do them anymore. If I couldn't be free to run and skip and climb and swing, I wouldn't do anything. It just wasn't fair.

In a very bad mood, I started down the trail that led away from the creek bank. I had never traveled down it before because my mom and dad said that it was too dangerous for young turtles. Turtles had to be near the water's edge, they said, so that if danger came they could dive and hide among the rocks or water plants. Well, I hadn't seen any danger. If anyone wanted my "motor home" they were welcome to it. It sure was nothing more than a nuisance to me.

The trail was bumpy and I was pitifully slow. I walked and walked and still was so close to the creek that I could hear the gurgling of the water and the crying of the water birds.

"Boy, am I slow," I reminded myself. "If it wasn't for this shell I could travel lots faster. Why, I'll bet I could run as fast

as a rabbit."

Just then I heard a noise behind me and I stretched out my neck and looked back. There was Woodie scurrying along after me. It made me even angrier. That's what it was to have a friend. You could *never* seem to get away from him.

"Po," he called. "Po, wait up."

"What are you doing out here?" I yelled back angrily. "Don't you know that this is a dangerous part of the woods?"

"I know," panted Woodie. "I know—so stop, will you?"

I stopped and waited. Woodie came puffing up beside me. He was just as slow as I was. But then he was another turtle—he had a shell slowing him down, too.

"So why are you following me?" I asked him rather angrily.

"I'm not following you—really, I—I just thought—well Flip thought—I mean—well, Flip sent me," he answered, his head down.

"Flip sent you?"

"He said—well, he said that he thought that you—that you might need a friend to talk to."

"Then why didn't he come?" I challenged.

"Oh, he would have—I mean, he said—well he thought that you'd maybe rather talk to me. Cause. Cause we—," began Woodie slowly, "he said that he wasn't sure if you'd want to talk to him—about—things—and me being your best friend, he thought that you might—"

"Okay, okay," I said, realizing that it was useless arguing over it. "You're here." I was still puzzled over Flip sending Woodie. Did it mean that Flip—? But Woodie was talking again.

"Where you going?" he puffed.

"Out," I said.

"Out where?"

"Who cares—just out."

"But it's dangerous," he cautioned. "You just said so yourself."

"Woodie," I said, "grow up, will you? All our life we've been told that it's dangerous—dangerous how? Have you ever heard of anyone going into these woods and not coming out?"

"Well,—no. But that doesn't mean—"

"Aw, cut it out," I broke in. "Now what could happen to a person out here anyway?"

"My dad says that there are animals in these woods who eat young turtles," said Woodie stubbornly. As he said it he looked nervously over his shoulder.

A new hope flickered in me. "You mean they might eat my shell?"

"Po," said Woodie in exasperation, "from what I've heard, your *shell* is the only part of you that they *won't* eat."

It wasn't fair. It just wasn't fair. Even the wild animals in the forest didn't want anything to do with my shell.

"Come back, will you Po?" Woodie was pleading.

"No," I told him. "I'm not going back. Not until I've found some way to get rid of this miserable, rotten, stifling shell."

"You can't get rid of your shell. It's part of you. That's the way we're made. It's the way—"

But I stopped Woodie. "Don't you see what it's doing to me," I cried. "It keeps me from having fun. I can't do any of the things that I want to do. There it is all the time, hanging right there on me, hemming me in, stopping all the—"

"Po," cut in Woodie. "You're no different than the rest of us. We all have shells, too."

"See," I said as though Woodie had proved my very point. "So what are you going to do about them?"

"Do about them? Well, nothing. Accept them. Accept them as part of me. That's just the way it is. There's no use fighting it. It won't change anything."

I turned from Woodie. I was even angrier now. "Okay," I yelled at him. "Okay, if you're satisfied with being tied to that extra baggage all the time, then fine! Go back! Me, I'm going looking for some answers."

I started off down the path. Without even turning around I knew that Woodie hadn't moved. He was still sitting there watching me go, and maybe there were tears running down his cheeks. Well, I didn't care, I was sick and tired—

A quick movement beside the trail caught me off guard. Something much bigger than I snatched me up, threw me in the air, then let me drop with a *thud,* and using a long, pointed nose, rolled me around on the ground. Then, before I could even gather my thoughts, sharp teeth sank into my right front leg and I heard Woodie screaming, "Tuck in, Po! Tuck in!" I pulled myself within my shell as far as I could pull.

It seemed forever that the strange "something" was rolling me back and forth, this way and that, pawing me, sniffing me, digging away at my shell, but I just curled up tighter. I had never been so scared in all of my life. Would my shell be strong enough to keep out the sharp teeth and avoid the hungry mouth? I pulled myself as deeply within my shell as I could. It was all that I could do.

After what seemed like hours, the strange creature, whatever it was, gave an angry "woof," threw me aside, and left me there where I had fallen. I still didn't dare to stick my head out. What if it was still around? Besides, I was on my back. I just hated to be on my back! Already I was dizzy and feeling sick to my stomach from it. I was afraid to stick out my legs and kick for fear I would bring the sharp-toothed animal back again. I just laid there, shivering and shaking and feeling mighty thankful for the protection of my shell. Why, if it hadn't been for my shell—I didn't even want to think about it.

A gentle nudge pushed at me and a whispering voice said, "Po, Po. Are you okay?"

It was Woodie. Never had anyone's voice been as welcome as Woodie's was to me now.

I stuck my head out just a bit. "Yeah," I said. "Yeah, I'm okay. Help me flip over, will you?"

I was soon on my feet again. It felt good to know down from up.

"Boy," said Woodie. "Boy, I was scared. I thought he had you, Po. Boy, if it wouldn't have been for your shell—"

"Yeah," I responded. "I know. We're just mighty lucky to have them, aren't we? They sure do come in handy when you need them." I laughed, a very shaky laugh.

"What we gonna do now?" asked Woodie, nervously checking over his shoulder again. I felt pretty nervous myself.

"I don't know about you," I said, "but I'm gonna get this

"motor home" of mine out of these woods and back to the creek just as fast as I can."

Woodie grinned. "Me, too," he agreed.

The nearer we got to the creek the better I felt. When my heart finally stopped its wild thumping, I was able to start thinking again. I thought mostly of what had just happened to me—and of what could have happened. I realized that I had a lot to be thankful for.

First of all, I was thankful for my good, strong shell—my crazy, clinging, cumbersome "motor home." It had saved my life. Boy, if I had been a rabbit or a squirrel, or a bird, or even a frog, I'd have been a goner for sure.

Then I was thankful for friends—friends who cared enough to worry about a guy when he was down. Friends like Woodie—and Flip. Flip? It was funny about Flip. He might be my toughest competition but he was something more, too. He was a real good friend.

"Woodie," I said suddenly as we scrambled toward the creek. "What would you think of making Flip our new leader?"